An American Beelzebub

Darby Guise

Bear Skin Bob Press

Also by Darby Guise

The Drunk'unn Boat

Harmony in Bad Taste

An American Beelzebub

An American Beelzebub

For he did not seem to know any way to do a person a
kindness but by killing them.

—Mark Twain, *The Mysterious Stranger*

1

He knew he should become his own teacher. That much had always been clear to him. He'd woken from a dream. In it, he was burnt and charred, beaten and whipped; the sun was blue; his skin was leathery and mutilated; he overlapped with wounds. His face was no longer human; amphibious overtones lurked amongst its conical shape; his family watched him. They saw what he'd become, something ghastly, instilling tears in his poor mother's eyes and revulsion in his father's gaze. His brother simply wept, and this was their reunion. The dream alluded to time only vaguely, and the duration of his captivity was unknown. He walked past his mother, each step painful and slow; there was nothing to say, and he crept forward and ventured out and looked on at the world; standing at the top of the steps of a great stone precipice, he raised his arms and stretched his lips across the horn of his beak—conjuring something new, something still without name. He spit blood and started downward.

2

He was seated on a toilet reading the graffiti left behind by some literate vandal.

"Enlightenment was just seeing how silly the whole thing was. How silly was enlightenment?" thought Richard.

He was a composition of matter seeking other matter, expunging matter, consuming matter, wondering, "What was the matter?"

Dick believed that a certain amount of suffering was required each day. It was part of his soul's gastrointestinal process.

The words were written on a swinging metallic door of a middling bathroom stall. Minutes later, he lit a cigarette and rolled down the car window; he hummed a tune; the sun cast its rays unimpeded, and the clock said 11 a.m.

3

The only thing he was serious about was his own self-derangement. Little else held sway over him. He was thirty-two years old. Christ was roughly that age when he'd died; Mozart was dead at thirty-five, Jesse James at thirty-four. He figured it was time he quit fooling around and grabbed what was rightfully his—pulled the rabbit from the hat, so to speak. He was off to visit an old friend. A man who'd once been prominently paraded as a mystic or seer or soothsayer of some renown, but due to a singular bout of well-documented madness (some twenty years before) when he'd proudly proclaimed a common sheep to be the reincarnation of some Slavic god, he'd lost all clout and credibility. He'd shown up muttering and screaming with his arms snug around the sheep's neck—a horrible burn on the back of his hand. A lone priest had tried to calm and pacify the brainsick fellow, and Frank had struck him, pummeled him with his fists. Rumors circulated (even alluding to relations between the pair), and ever since, he'd sheltered himself in a cloistered hut among the rolling hills, the waving terrain spanning for miles. Jebediah pulled up and walked the gravel path and knocked on the door.

The old man looked weak—thick glasses and a stodgy gait slowly making their way towards the screen door.

"Time has a way of dulling even the most abrasive surfaces. It's infallible, a great vat of acid; everything drifts and disintegrates; everything passes through its toxic clutches. A river of destruction that flows both ways."

Frank wandered over to his bookshelf and grabbed a deck of cards stuffed between two heavily bound books. He sat across from Jebediah, and his black and bony hands shuffled the deck—the familiar routine, and then he flipped the first card over.

Frank's deck wasn't your everyday, numinous deck; it had its own brand of peculiarities as Frank had crafted each of the cards himself. Hand-painted and worked out by some demented dream logic. The first card was the Headsman: the Headless Hessian himself, the hardened brute nourished by decapitations, the frontrunner of any and every battle, and a grim sign of the carnage to come.

"If you regretted everything until your very last moment and were then miraculously grateful (for all of it) right at the bitter end (in that final instant), would all regret that came before be negated? Or put another way, how redeeming is redemption?"

The next card laid down was the King. Unlike most iterations of the archetypical King, Frank's deck had him dressed as a pauper. Painted with poverty and madness, the frozen mannerisms of the King mid-jig only underlined his freakish nature. A dancing fool and outlier and yet, still, the King.

"A man's birth marks the first tumble of the very first domino, and—from there—all else is presaged and concrete, fixed and impermeable. All destinies are written in the first breath: all else is the consequence."

The third card was without name. It had a picture of a vibrant red rose stuck in a mound of snow. Black skies and falling flakes. *What could this one mean?*

Frank stood up and walloped Jebediah on the head with a devastating blow from some blunt object, and Jebediah hit the table hard. He was out cold and had a magnificent and odd vision. He was in the middle of a temple, stone walls and vines with a bonfire at the center, pillars carved with cryptic bas-reliefs etched out the perimeter; Jebediah watched as people swarmed, throwing books into the fire and kindling the blaze. He saw a man weeping in the corner, making his way towards the fire, prostrate and defeated, crawling on all fours. The mob kicked him and laughed at him. He was pleading for something, but no one was listening; they stopped only to mock him and inflict more torment on the creature. He collapsed. A group standing in the back watched, outside the mob's grasp, dressed in tunics and robes—their cries muted by the noise, back against the wall. They were obviously sympathetic to the plight of the defeated man but dared not enter the scene. Jebediah made his way through the crowd and saw that they were all burning the same book: *The Chronicle of Young Satan*. He went to the fallen man and tried to get him on his feet, but the man refused to budge, and Jebediah asked him what was going on, and the man told him that he was the book's author. The mob was shattering the mirror he'd made for them. So be it, he said. And then he began to laugh, and as his volume rose, so too did his spirits, and he was soon up on his feet; laughing still harder, he joined in—fighting the mob to get ahold of his work, and when he'd recovered an armful of copies, he'd run to the fire and toss the books in. Laughing more and more as the mob began to cool itself, confused by what they were witnessing, they stood mute and dumb, uncertain what was going on. *This is not how this is supposed to play out*, thought many of them. The author, insane and roaring with laughter, kept on with his now solitary book-burning efforts. When he'd burned the final available copy, some of the crowd had dispersed, but many were still in attendance, glued to the scene, and the author looked up with eyes of love and spoke, "What should we burn next, comrades?"

When Jebediah came to, Frank handed him a cup of tea and an icepack. He asked whether Jebediah had seen any-thing, and Jebediah told him about his vision.

"Hmm," said Frank. "I think you need a new name, son."

"Yeah?"

"Yes... something with some flash. Some bite. A *new* numerical name."

He shook Frank's hand and thanked him. They embraced, and Jebediah got in his car; armed with a new title, a cryptic vision, and a vague allusion to future events, he drove off, baptized by his friend Frank, the prescient old tiger.

4

His journey was to be long, and he eyed a beautiful woman on the corner of the road and thought of well-built furniture, and then he thought of his mother and her grace, and he thought of good partners and sturdy birch trees. He stopped at a red light, and then a kid ran up to his window.

"If I find out I'm *him*"—he pointed to a fat fella in front of a drugstore window—"I'm gonna kill myself," said the kid.

What the hell? thought No. 44.

"What are you on about, child?"

"I said, 'If I was him"—he pointed again to the fat man (who stood looking at a crack in the glass pane) swaying slightly back and forth—"I'd end it all, do myself in,' and you know what, mister?"

"What?"

"I've been to heaven... and ain't a *goddamn* soul there."

$$5$$

Being pure evil, he understood the heart of the world—evil in this instance being comparable to a state of pure determination, not dogged by guilt, not wavering with multiple intents, singular and blind and focused. A will to survive. A will with a why. A will to power—and with each idea formed, a microcosm of that will exposes itself to the world. The battle of wills is the battle of ideas, and the battle of ideas is predicated on the fervor and tenacity of wordplay, evolving of its own accord, surviving and spreading among the speakers and hosts of languages and tongues. Combatants existing and battling and failing and joining and disintegrating. Lying in wait in books and computer screens, air raids exiting mouths and megaphones—the organism of words and the macrocosm of concepts. *This was quite a battleground,* thought Jeb. Civility was a dead dog, and trench warfare reigned supreme. No. 44 was welcomed back to the world as he bought a pack of cigarettes and lit up outside a convenience store. ("Got a light?" asked a homeless man, and No. 44 offered his flame.)

His intuition compelled him to go to the pool hall, and his legs abided.

6

He shot the balls around for over an hour before someone came over and asked if he wanted to partake in a friendly competition—$50 a game. Sure, said No. 44, and their game began, and No. 44 lost handily and with it, fifty bucks.

Game two begins; this one happens in much the same fashion as the one that came before it. The third and fourth and fifth are in the same vein as their predecessors, but on the sixth—and $250 in the hole—No. 44 starts unraveling impossible shots in an unruly game plan that just edges out his opponent. Pure luck, says the other fellow upon his very first loss, and game seven begins. The gloves are off.

By the end of the afternoon, No. 44 was up $600; he walked out grinning like an idiot; he went over to the bar across the street and grabbed himself a whiskey. The place was rustic and unbothered, only a sparse clientele this early in the day. He sat at the bar and drank his drink. A woman edged over towards him in between songs and asked, "What are you all about, mister?"

Soon, two others appeared; they introduced themselves. The Sisters of Mercy was their preferred handle. A trio of female musicians and they invited him over to their place (a short walk away). Why not? said No. 44, and he drank up the last of his whiskey and followed the ladies out.

Outside, he saw his opponent from the pool hall smoking freebase cocaine from a small green pipe. The sun was making its descent; all was quiet on the Western Front.

7

The Sisters of Mercy lived in what appeared to be a shack in a heavily wooded area that arose from nowhere. They were walking down the street, chatting and passing businesses and shops, and they darted down a narrow alleyway, a dirt path with an opening of only a few small feet. Soon they were pushing branches out of the way, and No. 44 could hear a creek or river or water flowing from some nearby source; he asked the ladies how much farther, and one of them pointed her finger and said, "That's it."

The house was constructed from odds and ends; plywood and tin were unscrupulously hammered and bent together to bring this bastard to life. Smoke was exiting the chimney, and a string operated the front door. The house protruded out at odd angles, an architectural design bordering on parody, and inside, draped with an assortment of quilts and rugs and lit by an arsenal of lamps, was a decidedly elegant interior—strangely inviting—and although small, it captivated with its many dimensions. The Sisters told him that they lived out here for a variety of reasons, mainly so they could practice and sing their songs unbothered. Out here, they were alone. No. 44 asked if they'd play him a tune, and the gals agreed, and they began by harmonizing their voices, and one of them grabbed a pair of sticks and bounced them off the walls and tables and lampshades, and another grabbed a violin and started in on it, and a song came to life. A spell was born, and No. 44 sat down on an ugly, old couch and listened to the ladies play their tune.

The song was beautiful (wrenching loose sections of No. 44's soft and sentimental side); teardrops ran down his cheeks, and when they finished and saw No. 44's face, one of them came over and softly blotted out his tears and kissed him, and then another came by and placed a mask on his head, and the other bent low and started fondling his junk, and, from there, the foursome entered into an unusual sensual pact as exploratory efforts were carried out, and No. 44 and the Sisters of Mercy probed and stroked and licked and fucked their way to sunup. No. 44 woke up first, limbs from the ladies draped over him every which way. He sauntered over to the mirror. A naked man with a latex mask, he growled and hissed and stirred up another erection and wandered back to the ladies and woke one of them up; they fucked vigorously and with great verve. And then she came, and then he came, and he got dressed and growled one last time at the ladies, two of whom were still fast asleep as the other lay still, sweating with a smirk; she blew him a kiss, and he only removed the mask outside, and he placed it on a knobbly branch near the shack's entrance. The mask hung limp, the snout now comical without any blood or bone beneath to give it life.

8

People had trouble with him. He was liable to be... unorthodox.

9

Does God punish beauty? He was mulling this over as he edged his old Buick out onto the street and exited the town and set off on the highway—soon entering desert terrain. He stopped to get gas, and when he checked his wallet, he realized he was $200 short. The Sisters had taken their cut, and although he cursed them, he quickly got over it and sipped his coffee and smoked his cigarette and drove on and turned up the radio. The weatherman told him that the day was going to be hot. A hitchhiker with long, scraggly hair stood lonesome on the side of the road, and No. 44 pulled over to let him in.

"Hop in, partner."

He placed his sack in the back seat and sat shotgun and told Jeb about his adventures. The hitchhiker was traveling northbound, headed to Alaska. No. 44 could only take him a short way as their paths would soon diverge, but the hitchhiker was happy to be edged along (even just a little bit farther).

No. 44 dropped him off at a service station full of big rigs and semi-trucks and bought the kid a meal at the restaurant inside. The hitchhiker was from Wyoming, and No. 44 asked him about Old Faithful and the Devils Tower, and the hitch-hiker told him that the real show was the Grand Prismatic Spring. And No. 44 asked him what was in Alaska, and he said solitude and nature and peace. And No. 44 asked him why he had to travel so far for these things when they could be found and experienced and bought right here, and the hitchhiker shrugged and said that his gut told him to go north, and No. 44 had no answer to that. He paid the boy's bill and wished him luck and drove off into the night.

He pulled off the road an hour later and stopped at a biker bar. He played pool and won $100 and got drunk and passed out in his back seat and woke up deranged and thirsty. He knocked on the bar's door, trying to get water, but no one was there, and he wandered around back and drank from a spigot, and then he drove through the desert canyons and pulled over at some point to puke—and then he kept on keeping on, forward and weaving, bobbing and flowing with the pavement as it cut its way through the land.

10

Her name was Norma. He saw her sitting outside her room, adjacent to his. He eyed her at the pool too, floating on an inflatable lounger with a convenient cup holder. Her purple top and matching bottoms exposed a beautiful woman in her late twenties. She wore sunglasses, and No. 44 was only privy to the nectar of her eyes—in all their glory—later that evening, when they sat outside discussing this and that over cold beers at a poolside table.

Who was Norma? A woman of distinguished stature, she was visiting her mother and sister, and she chose to settle here for a month or so. Living out on the limits of town and enjoying the company of lackadaisical days and cool, lonely evenings. She said that No. 44 was a welcome addition to her routine and that whenever she felt bored or tired or in need of change, something would always turn up; it was the way of the motel. Through a revolving door of guest stars emerged one or two interesting sorts, enough to appease her social appetites and her enigmatic, lustful ways (which popped up

from time to time, sometimes dormant for months, then—
Bam! horny and in heat). No. 44 enjoyed Norma's company,
and—as the sun set and the neon glow of the Regal Raven
illuminated the night sky—she touched his hand and stared
into his eyes and led him into her room, and No. 44 was
exhilarated by her rhythmic moans and pulsating pelvis,
and they laughed and smoked and talked and slept, and
when he got up, he kissed her and wandered back to his
room and slept for another few hours before getting down
to brass tacks.

The thing that No. 44 found the most ridiculous was that
given enough pain, eventually it all becomes comical—and
then he stubbed his toe on the corner of the dresser and
cursed and blasphemed the Lord's name: *such is man's
existence*, he thought.

He had a hatchet that he kept in his trunk. It was his
weapon of choice. The proper weight and balance for his
doings. When was the last time he'd dispatched someone?
It'd been a while. He needed a reason, not necessarily a good
one, but one that would superficially hold up—at least temporarily and to mild scrutiny. He saw a kid bully another
kid at the pool and thought him too young, and then he
saw the bully be bullied by his overweight father, stationed
a couple of units down, room 119, and figured that he might
do, but then he thought about the kid (already, presumably,
on a bad path) and how he might go from bad to worse
after seeing his father brutally murdered seemingly without
reason or motive. He wasn't in the business of creating
violent prototypes or sowing the path for future murderous
little tyrants; he was in the business of killing though, and he
waited eagerly for his workload to arrive. And then, lo and

behold, the clouds parted and his telephone rang, and he was given a name: Lucas Basson—five thousand dollars and to be completed within two days. No. 44 asked what he'd done, and the voice said he was a former member of the Brothers Beelzebub who'd defected. Fair enough, said No. 44. He was given the address (a day's drive away), and a picture of Lucas was sent to his phone; he paid for his room and left. He saw Norma at the pool, and he waved, but she didn't see him.

When he pulled up to the house, it was 6 p.m., and he put on his gloves and got out his hatchet, and he knocked on the door, and the man from the photo answered, and No. 44 said "Lucas," and the man said, "That's right," and No. 44 slammed the hatchet into his face and pushed him inside. He shut the door and delivered a couple more good whacks, and then No. 44 took out his phone and sent a text declaring the deed done; he went to the kitchen and grabbed a snack and stepped over the body and left. He felt good, and the evening was sunny with a cool breeze. He lit a cigarette and drove on. He received a text ("payment deposited"); then he stopped at a steakhouse to eat, and while he waited for his food, he took out a pen and drew on the tablecloth, and the waitress said, "Sorry, sir, you can't do that," but she was too late—the deed had already been done.

He got another call the next day; it'd woken him up; he'd slept in his car. It wasn't one of his usual callers, and No. 44 demanded to know who it was. And then the voice revealed some of his secrets, *dark secrets*, things he didn't know anyone else knew. Who was this? Was this some ham-fisted attempt at blackmail? Was he being strong-armed into some new hell? Some new bidding? The voice said it had an assignment for him: one hundred names in need of cancelation. For each name crossed off, he'd receive ten thousand in change. Payment was issued upon completion of each job, but as an act of good faith, they'd paid for the first kill up front. "Who are you?" asked No. 44, and the voice said that the less he knew, the better. He agreed to the contract, having no other plans and nothing else better to do, and he was told to drive to Fort Worth, Texas (6782 Riverbend Drive). When he got there, someone would give him a list, and he should start from the top and work his way down. The order was important, and he must execute each kill by his own hand (those were the rules), and No. 44 said okay. He hung up and rerouted his route; he was Texas bound.

11

When he got to 6782 Riverbend Drive, it turned out to be a quaint little bungalow with a flourishing garden out front. The house looked thirty or forty years old but was well kept, and the neighborhood held large, brooding trees adorning front lawns and backyards, providing shape and contour and history to the area. No. 44 knocked at the front door, and a little old lady opened it and beckoned him inside. She brought him tea and cookies and told him of the weather. Hot, she said. She drifted on about her rheumatism and spoke casually of the Lord and His bountiful offerings, and then she handed No. 44 an envelope, and he opened it while sitting on the loveseat. It was *The List*—typed up in sans-serif font, one hundred deep, with the first name bearing the title "Julie Johannasson." The old lady asked if he'd like to stay for dinner, and he agreed, and he helped her set the table, and then he sat listening to the old woman as she prepared their victuals. "Hmm, delicious," he said, as he stabbed and cut and skewered cabbage rolls and sausages and perogies and shoved them into his mouth.

After supper, the old woman told him she needed to visit her neighbor and to come along, and he agreed without hesitation. They shuffled out together as the old woman clung to his arm, and they made their way from one front lawn to the next. They rang the bell, and a woman in her early forties appeared at the door.

"Mrs. Willoughby, to what do I owe the pleasure?"

Mrs. Willoughby snickered, as if being addressed in this manner tickled her funny bone, and then she made a somewhat nonsensical noise (a booger popped out from her nose but was rapidly sucked back in), and then she said, "I wanted to introduce you to my friend. Ms. Julie Johannasson, this is No. 44."

Julie invited them in, and they sat in her living room and talked about this and that. Mrs. Willoughby mentioned the garden and the weather and their pain-in-the-ass neighbor Jerry. All the while, No. 44 was mulling over Julie, this figure before him, this easy-going missus. What kind of list was this? Was this a setup? Some punchline to some obscure joke? *Death to the suburban class*! She was, by all accounts, a decent and kind individual, but her name was most assuredly at the top of the list. Perhaps she was some horrible deviant or a witness of some kind—too dangerous and knowledgeable to live. In reality, it didn't matter much, he had a job to do, and he'd go about it one way or another. The reasons were not his to worry about. Mrs. Willoughby excused herself and went to the bathroom, and No. 44 sat in awkward silence until Julie piped up.

"So, you're here to do me in, eh?"

"Huh?" said No. 44.

"I just wanted to say... *thank you*. There's a gun under the cushion."

No. 44 reached his hand under the cushion and retrieved a silenced pistol. She smiled at him. He smiled back. He leveled the gun and fired.

When Mrs. Willoughby came back from the bathroom and saw No. 44 with the gun and Julie with the bullet in her head, she said, "Good gracious, look at this mess. Well, dear, you go on now; you've plenty of work to do. We'll clean this up, and we'll be in contact with you over the next couple of days. Take care, hon."

No. 44 stumbled out of the house and made his way back to his car. He retrieved the list from his pocket and crossed out Julie's name; the next name on the list was Philip Baker. *Who are these people?* One hundred souls in line for a swift dispatch, what was the link that brought them together, consolidated them on a single portable document? Perhaps the mystery would become clearer as he progressed through it—or perhaps not. He thought it strange that she knew he was coming. Was this some voluntary kill list? A suicidal pact with some devil? A one-way trip precipitated by his gun and hatchet, freeing the soul from the confines of flesh and blood by their own consenting volition? A ritual? Voluntary euthanasia?

Nope... at least not in Philip Baker's case. He ran with all his might once he saw No. 44 and his little red hatchet.

Philip lived in Fort Worth too, on the opposite side of town. Mrs. Willoughby had given him directions, and he'd gone to the house that very same night. When he'd crept inside, he fell, tripping over a side table, exhibiting all the grace of a handicapped hog, waking Philip up, and No. 44

had to chase him around the house, a naked and terrified man, and force him to show some ID (to be sure of who he was). Philip was fearful and chaotic right until the bitter end—the complete opposite of Julie Johannasson. He slept on Philip's couch that night and got up the next day before the sun had risen; he ate two Pop-Tarts and stepped over the corpse and drove off in search of the third name on the list: Martha Hatchford.

12

Denise Sinclair was a spry eight-year-old. She was the fifth name on the list. *What the hell*? He'd driven to Canada— Montreal, to be exact. He'd taken his time driving north across the States. Having already dispatched four names in less than two weeks, he was well ahead of schedule, and he decided to take in some of the sights along his journey. He listened to Ween's *Chocolate and Cheese* (humming along to the tune of "Spinal Meningitis") and ate garbage food along the highway. He entertained himself with small-town attractions (strange sculptures and measly fairs), and when he got to Montreal and found her house (each name had a code beside it that could be entered into an online database with information about the target's address and photos and presumed whereabouts based on known routines and presupposed timelines (he only found out about this later... after he'd killed the fourth name; his phone rang, and the voice finally told him about it; before, he'd simply stalked their social media accounts and proceeded through trial and error (he'd already killed one person by accident who wasn't on the list))), he wasn't sure if he could do it. The entire journey had him going over the pros and cons of taking Denise Sinclair's life. He didn't need the money, but there was a good chance his employers would kill him if he didn't complete his mission (a rogue agent was never good for business), but even that didn't seem to concern him all that much. What really irked him was leaving the task unfinished. He wasn't the type of fella to leave things undone—especially when his heart was in it (or his will, at any rate), and the wheels were turnin', and the tread dug in. Everything needed to be completed once it'd been started. (*Even if it involves killing innocent little girls?* he asked himself.) He supposed he could make it quick, take her out while she was sleeping so she didn't have any fear or hurt or pain as she departed this plane for whatever was next. He took a long drag of his cigarette and eyed a vacant teeter-totter across the street moving up and down of its own accord.

13

If No. 44 had read the Bible, he'd have known that God sometimes kills whole clusters of children just because.

14

He'd been living and traveling on his own for years now, mostly living out of his car and only coming into contact with an old acquaintance or friend (scattered at random across the landscape) every couple of years or so. If he told people how he lived, even vaguely, coated in foggy details and half-truths, they still had a hard time believing him. They looked at his austere lifestyle or ascetic ways or vagabond wanderings as childish and without purpose; they could not see the bigger picture, the larger design. Too fixed on details to properly pull focus and allow the world to make sense, even for one brief moment. It was disgust that drove him here. Disgust with people, disgust with the world—disgust with himself (any outward emotion is generally a reflection of an internal one), and the disgust Jebediah Wells felt sunk him, and he drifted—away from people—and in his seclusion, he found hope and solitude and happiness (or whatever happiness he felt available to him). And it was while reviewing these thoughts that he climbed Denise Sinclair's tree house and opened her window and aimed his gun and shot the sleeping child.

He got back in his car and crossed out the fifth name. He thought of Joan of Arc and Gilles de Rais.

15

He still had ninety-five to go. Wow, this was quite an undertaking. He wondered if the cops were hot on his trail, but the breadth and distance between killings (apart from the first two) seemed to offer him some cover, but even he, diligent and skilled assassin, was sure to pique the suspicion and curiosity of some random citizen or curious law-enforcement type at some point. Someone was bound to see him leveling his gun or hatchet, coming out of some abode covered from tip to boot in blood. And then there were the cameras—perpetuated and populated at almost every street corner. The world loved to record, from trivial morning monologues to random street-side violence, the carnival had taken over its own programming, and reality and fiction were converging into one ridiculous show, bleeding and mixing into itself, creating a magnificent, fucked-up kaleidoscope of daydreams and conceits which No. 44 was quite content to be inhabiting. *It wasn't all bad*, he thought. To be privy to watching the world burn in small clumps and big swaths and care little for how the debris settled. One had to be amoral in times like these. Death was natural and chaos the norm, who cared if the whole thing were to explode and annihilate itself right here and now. Perhaps jubilation would accompany destruction, and the moment of extermination would be the greatest triumph.

The next kill was a man named George Peterson (a small balding man). He tied George up in his home, and George called him a coward and a weakling, and No. 44 asked him what he could do to assuage this low opinion George had of him, and he said, "Fucking *kill* yourself." And No. 44 laughed and told him he couldn't do that, but he'd purposefully injure himself for George's enjoyment if he liked. He took out his hatchet (not waiting for George's response) and raised it and brought it down, chopping off his pinkie and his ring finger—splitting each digit just above the knuckle of his left hand. He screamed in pain and laughed between sobs and punched the table and screamed some more. *What a stupid idea*, thought No. 44. He was bleeding all over the place, and instead of instilling enjoyment in George, he seemed to have rendered disgust and fear in him. He dispatched his captive with a quick bullet to the head and picked up his fingers and drove to the hospital. They were only able to reattach the one, but he kept his pinkie anyway. And while driving out of town, he tossed his amputated morsel to a feral carnivore wandering the night streets; the cat put it in its mouth and carried it down the alleyway and out of sight.

16

He was strategically forgetful, one of his many superpowers, enabling him to do horrendous and tremendous things without ever having remembered doing them. This kept him sane in an otherwise insane brain. Memory would have certainly been his undoing—good thing he had the list to keep him honest. Number 7 was located on the other side of Canada, in Alberta, and No. 44 drove westward through the prairies and wheat fields. He enjoyed the flat terrain, the uniformity of it. At a gas station, he chatted amicably with the owner, and they discussed the little-known eccentricities of the area. The owner introduced himself as Pete Thomsdale. *Where had No. 44 seen that name before?* And then he drove off, and a mile or two down the road, he remembered, and he grabbed the list, and, sure as shit, ol' Pete's name was squarely written in the thirty-fourth slot. No. 44 pulled a U-turn and went back, and Pete smiled as he saw him advance, and No. 44 raised his gun and dumbfounded Pete just stood there. And just as he was about to pull the trigger, his phone rang, and No. 44 told Pete to sit down and shut up. He answered the call, and the voice said to follow the list, never deviate from the order—and No. 44 said that the order was cramping his style and becoming a real pain in his ass, and the voice repeated the command, and No. 44 said okay.

He tied Pete's hands with an extension cord, and they drove off into the prairies, and Pete asked him why he was doing this, and No. 44 just shrugged. And Pete offered to pay him a decent sum to let him go, but No. 44 didn't answer, and then he told Pete to shut up—and not wanting to let Pete stammer on any longer... or get all gooey-eyed about his inevitable demise, No. 44 decided to tell him a story.

The world is on the brink of collapse, only six people remain; they decide to band together in order to survive. The group consists of three men and three women. Things go smoothly in the beginning as they divvy up the tasks and develop into a tight-knit community, and time marches on. Eventually, one of the men and one of the women get together and have a child. They decide to move down the road and start a new life for themselves and separate from the group. Years go by, and eventually, they go back to the group, and they find that they too have propagated the species, and where there were once six, there are now nine. Time continues and the group grows. One night, celebrating the birthday of one of the children, they hear a noise in the forest, and before they can arm themselves and investigate, a pack of wolves enters into their camp and overruns them, and all but two aging men are killed. With no future or hope for humanity and only haunting memories of a lost chance torn away, their wills turn foul; they devise a pact and each goes in his own direction: one heads east and the other west. And their adventure is based on extermination. They wander the land killing everything they come in contact with, and God keeps them alive. He torments them with long lives and watches the fall of man precipitated in the fates of these two final antiheroes. And when both of these agents of destruction die and they are able to converse with God, they ask Him why He cursed them. And He replies, "Brothers of Job, I did no such thing. You are animals, and you have behaved as such. I cursed you no more than I did the wolves that ate your kin. They were hungry and reacted; you were despondent and did so too. Your pain and suffering are fictions based solely on your perspectives. You seek favoritism and answers as vanity blurs your thoughts. Does the cub that was eaten by its starving mother question the way of things? No, it dies in agony, alone, without ever seeking justice or understanding for the brutal act. Humans are unique in their need to understand suffering, even falsely, under the guise of self-deception. Every death is both senseless and necessary. The arrogance of man is what thrusts him upon the pedestal of erroneous worth. Mankind was an experiment in narcissism, and I cannot say that I'm not somewhat relieved to be done with him."

The story did not play well with the audience, and its ominous and dark closure alluded to what fate had in store for poor Pete, the agreeable everyman.

17

No. 44 got a call and was told of a place where he could take Pete and where one of the lieutenants of this mysterious and shadowy organization would manage and look after him until his number was called and his time was up. It was a small house with a long driveway and no other buildings for miles, and No. 44 took him inside, and a young girl (maybe sixteen) was there waiting for them.

"You're the lieutenant?" asked No. 44, surprised by the girl's youth.

"Yes, sir. Leave him, and when you get to his name, come back here, and I'll have him ready for you."

"Couldn't you just… you know, save me the hassle of coming all the way back and take care of *it* yourself?"

"I'm afraid it doesn't work like that, sir. It'll have to be you."

They got Pete inside, and the girl handcuffed him to the radiator, and he sat on the sofa, and he said, "Why me?" and the girl said, "Why not?" and Pete looked to No. 44 for help, and No. 44 just shook his head, and then Pete spoke again,

"But I'm a person. I have a family and a life. I don't deserve this."

"It has nothing to do with deserving," said the girl. "You think it's personal, Pete, but it's not. You're a product to be consumed at the right time. I'm sorry, but that's the way it is."

He quieted down, and No. 44 got up to leave, and just as he was exiting the door, the girl came over and handed him a .308 caliber rifle; he thanked her and placed the new hardware in his trunk and drove west to kill number 7.

18

He adopted God's sense of humor. This was his stroke of genius. Both destruction and creation were born of the same vein for him, equal in his eyes. Life no longer held any greater purpose than consuming itself and projecting that altered version forward. He readied his rifle and targeted number 7 (a shaggy-looking bastard named Darby) and pulled the trigger and blew off his head.

19

"Keep up or shut the fuck up!" The bum was yelling this at the crowd as No. 44 crossed the border and entered back onto American soil. A cop on a bicycle nodded to him as he drove past, and a billboard said, "He speaketh in tongues."

Ninety-three more, could this be? He seemed exhausted by the sheer daunting weight of the number, the duration required to attain that ripe and round triple-digit beast signifying completion: 100 kills. When facing such ridiculous, time-consuming, and gargantuan tasks, it was good to have a system that could be implemented to blind the worker, keep them focused on immediate and short-term goals, providing regular and much-needed hits of dopamine. Thus, No. 44 did his best to focus only on the next kill. He ceased to read further than the next name on the list, and this tactic proved to be helpful in keeping him sane and diligent.

20

Jerry Duvall was next. He was located in a town called Greywater, and No. 44 drove towards it. When he got there, he needed a break; he set the killings on pause for a bit; he parked his car and caught a movie at the local theater. It was a romantic comedy, just what he needed, something to counteract the debauchery and senseless violence that was accruing in his daily life. The movie held firm to the genre's tropes, and No. 44 walked out mildly refreshed—the happy ending and the ode to blossoming love made him crave ice cream, and he wandered down the street in search of his fix.

Waiting in line for his dipped cone and listening to the parlor's ode to classic rock 'n' roll, he bopped his foot to the beat. He heard someone yell after someone named Jerry. Could it be? And it was, and he shook his head and cursed the Fates. "Why can't you leave me alone with your goddamn coincidences and giftwrapped deliveries for one *goddamn* minute!?" No reply. And so, he followed the voice, and having already seen Jerry's photo, he knew that he'd already stumbled upon his target without ever having tried to. Jerry was with a woman, and No. 44 was more inclined than ever to limit the bloodshed, and he walked and waited behind the pair—eating his cone and biding his time.

Jerry walked the lady home, then proceeded alone and even cut through a dark and dingy alley (*could it be this easy?* thought No. 44, and sure enough, it was). He said, "Hey, Jerry," and Jerry turned, and No. 44 walked over to him, and just lying on top of a garbage lid was an ice pick, and so he picked it up and neared Jerry, and he thrust the pick through Jerry's jaw and punctured upward through his mouth, and then he retracted the instrument, and swung again, this time horizontally, and the pick went through his skull and into his brain—entering near his ear—and down went Jerry.

He kept the ice pick and went back to his car and found lodging in a decent motel not too far. No. 44 sprawled out on the bed and watched TV. He wondered about the ease of his task, the way it presented itself to him—as if he couldn't fail. He wondered if he was getting ahead of himself, if these were not the rambling of a (up until now) lucky egoist. Words from a black-and-white western rang out from the TV. "*Some are born to sweet delight. Some are born to endless night.*"

21

He decided to stay in Greywater the next day. It was a lovely little town. A blossoming garden grove decorated the main square, and cobblestone streets departed from its heart, and No. 44 spent the morning walking around and window gazing and browsing an outdoor market. He bought a newspaper and saw that his actions from the night before had found the front page. "Local Man, Jerry Duvall, Murdered in Alleyway." One night in town and already making headlines—*not bad*, thought No. 44.

He didn't do much that day. He mostly just sat around his motel room and watched TV. He ventured out to the pool for an hour, but an overly talkative woman nearing the end of her days wouldn't shut up, and this peeved him, and he went back to his room to escape her idiotic banter.

When night fell upon the scene, No. 44 felt like going out. A good meal and a night of frivolous entertainment sounded good; maybe he'd find a pool hall or a bowling alley to whittle away the hours. He showered and dug out an old, musty suit from his trunk and powdered his nose; he emerged a dapper man. He asked the front desk for any recommendations, and the old man told him to head two blocks east; there, he'd find what he was looking for.

He started eastward, and a large neon arrow animated its way downward towards a handleless steel door. He knocked, and then he heard someone move towards the peephole and eye him from the other side.

"What do you want, mister?"

"Hmm... to come in, I suppose."

"You got money?"

"Oodles."

He heard the door unlatch, and the steel monolith swung open, and No. 44 was admitted into a large ballroom (decorated in the style of a 1920s Parisian café). No. 44 was beside himself with pleasure, and a man ushered him to a small table with a decent view of the stage; he ordered a whiskey and some mussels, and he sat quietly as the lights dimmed, and the focus of the room was directed at the altar.

A woman appeared and walked aggressively back and forth onstage, leering at the audience. She was scantily dressed (wearing leather garb) with swaths of paint adorning her face; she furrowed her brow at her onlookers.

"I am woman, hear me roar! I am *wooomaaaaaaannnn*, hear me roar!"

She repeated this maxim and kept up with the attitude as a waiter brought No. 44 his drink and prepped his table for the upcoming meal. He heard orchestrations and looked up; a band had miraculously appeared onstage—a trombone, an upright bass, drums. The woman screamed, and the band kicked off, and a booming riff echoed through the salon, and the lively chorus sent tantalizing shivers through No. 44 as his mussels arrived, and he dug in.

He met a woman that night seated at the bar. She was beautiful with her hair held up in a loose updo and a shimmering dress displaying narrow shoulders below an elegant nape. She asked him what he did, and he said he was in construction, and she said he was lying, and he said maybe. They went back to her place and made love, and in the morning, he left and hopped on a bus, and the man next to him commented on his wrinkled suit and alluded to his "walk of shame," and No. 44 corrected him and said it was his plod of victory. The man laughed nervously, and No. 44 picked a booger from his nose and flicked it at him.

That was all it took for him to get back on track. A reset button, a good night of carefree sex and a scrumptious meal, and then it was back to business. He took out the list, and next to number 9 was the word "Wayne."

22

He looked up Wayne in the database and found out that he or she or it was a shark. *What the hell*? It was a great white—and its only definable characteristic separating it from the rest of its species (at least in No. 44's eyes) was a long scar scraping across its nose. Was he to kill a shark now? What the *hell* kind of list was this? And how was he supposed to hunt, find, and kill this beast? Did they know he hated water?

He dialed *69 on his phone and got the mysterious stranger on the other end.

"What is it?"

"I'm supposed to kill a *fucking* shark?"

"Yes."

No. 44 paused; for some reason he had expected the voice to atone for the error, assuage his anger, curse the stupidity of the list, and apologize to No. 44 for this moronic and juvenile prank. But it was no prank. This was his task—100 kills: man, woman, beast, or what-have-yous. He hung up and took a good look at the database. The shark (or Wayne) was over on the Atlantic Coast near Maine. He sat back on the bed and realized he needed another night of frivolous fun before he embarked on this *ridiculous* goddamn shark hunt and drove all the way across the country—once again.

He decided to strut back to the same haunt as the night before.

He knocked at the steel door again. This time, the arrow overhead wasn't lit, and when the voice on the other side asked him what he wanted, he said, "To come in," and the door opened, and the large doorman was holding a knife. He told No. 44 to hold out his hands, and No. 44 obliged, and the doorman cut across one of his palms and told him to smear the blood on the large stone with strange markings stationed where only yesterday a hostess stand had been. He did as he was told, and the usher—now wearing a golden baby mask—handed him a napkin and took him to his seat.

No one came to take his order, but a plate of sausage and sauerkraut and dumplings arrived at his table. He dug in, famished as he was, but he couldn't help but note that something seemed a little off from the traditional recipe.

The woman from the night before took the stage. She was wearing a red cape wrapped around her body, and her face was painted in a new configuration. The lights dimmed, and she started to scream, and she ran amok—back and forth—in a craze. A naked man wearing the head of a bull came on-stage with one of the biggest penises No. 44 had ever seen. He chased the woman and smacked her with an open hand, and she screamed, and she went down, and he hit her again. He punched her in the stomach, the eyes of the beast fixed and unmoving. He tore off her cape to reveal her naked porcelain body, and he began pumping away at his penis while he held her head with the other hand—squeezing her jaw between his thumb and forefinger—forcing her terrified gaze towards his beastly dome, and she fell back, and blood came pouring out from her nose. The beast got on top of her and forced her knees towards her head—exposing her genitalia his way. He rammed his member into her; the patrons watched mute. *Was this a show with consenting (albeit extremist) actors or a genuine hall of horrors?* thought No. 44. And then the room began to morph, and he looked to his left, and a giant reptile dressed in a red frock winked at him as her date bit into her neck, and then No. 44 took in the rest of his surroundings, and he saw a carnival of terror erupt as people were being eaten alive by giant reptilian beasts, and yet others were rolling in the intestines and mutilated flesh of their fellow guests (an orgy of bodily fluids), as one man ran jerking off, coming on an unsuspecting diner's hairpiece, but was soon decapitated by a sword-brandishing dyke in leather chaps. No. 44 sat still and watched the events play out as screams and moans erupted from every corner of the edifice, and a waiter bent down and started sucking him off, and the next thing he remembered, he was onstage with a sword, and he swung the goddamn thing, and he cut the bull-man's head clean off, and then he castrated the poor SOB and started fucking the once-caped woman as he whipped her as hard as he could with the bull-man's (dismembered) member.

23

He called the voice the next morning and told it about his night, and the voice told him that his food was probably laced with drugs (LSD? Adrenochrome?). They tended to mix the blood of an infant with desecrated wafers, stuffing it into meats and dumplings with heavy doses of psychoactive drugs. These were the victuals at a typical Black Mass nowadays, said the voice.

24

The conversation with the voice (their first in which No. 44 felt like they'd bonded somewhat) precipitated interest in the Black Mass, and No. 44 found himself online, investigating and browsing videos and blogs and channels and sites and getting lost in threads and thickets and muck and mutilated tidbits of proof with asinine comments and reconstructed theories, populated by some of the worst writers No. 44 had ever read—with tiny goldmines of knowledge with propulsive directions hidden here and there, functioning as the web's only silver lining. Hours went by; in the end, No. 44 felt like shit and decided the entirety of the internet, from tit to top, was a foul, toxic cesspool of mental waste and egoism—goddamn junk food. Fuck nuance! He'd nuke it if it were possible, go back in time and murder the son of a bitch who started it all.

He thought of Ted Kaczynski, and he calmed down.

25

Fun fact #12: No. 44 always preferred finding items to buying them—something to do with them lying in wait, his arrival prophesized in their collection. And when he opened his motel door that morning, ready to depart and head eastward to hunt that goddamn shark, he saw an old rusty chainsaw leaning up against the stucco siding below the window of his room. He inspected it and looked around, and no one seemed to be watching him. He opened the choke and pressed the fuel primer and pulled the cord and up started the machine. *A gift*, he thought, and No. 44 put the chainsaw in his trunk—his arsenal expanded: a rifle, a silenced pistol, a hatchet, an ice pick, and now, a chainsaw.

He drove east and cut in and out of various radio signals (a polyphony of radio waves, each combatting for the use of a single FM channel). In the end, he slipped in an old Hank Williams CD and whistled his way towards Maine.

Once there, No. 44 got a call, and the voice said, "You're gonna need a boat." And No. 44 said, "I sure as shit will."

And the voice told him to go to 67 Sunset Cove; a man named Jack was waiting for him. They had arranged for Jack to take him out, and he was told that ole Cap'n Jack was already privy to all the information he needed in order to help No. 44, and No. 44 said, "Okay," and hung up.

Jack was an unorthodox sort; he seemed to be missing random bits—e.g., half an ear lost, three fingers gone, a chunk torn out from his left calf—and he fidgeted and turned ungracefully and spoke in mutters and shouts, his eyes seemingly fixated on different points.

"No. 44! Is that you, boy?"

"Jack?"

"Yes, yes, that's me. Come aboard, lad. Time's a tickin'."

Jack didn't say much; he mostly just muttered to himself, tossing chum out in the open water as No. 44 sat back and toyed with his chainsaw. No. 44 didn't care much for Jack, but he liked that his deformed captain left him in peace. Something about his spastic ways bothered him, and he felt inclined to use his chainsaw to carve another piece from the already dwindling creature. No. 44 was sweating as the sun beat down, and he asked Jack if he had any sunscreen, and the captain told him to check the bin starboard side, and inside he found a dirt-ridden bottle of oily cream with stray hairs clinging to its plastic; he removed his shirt and slathered it on and sat back, taking in the foul smell of rotting chum and sickly sunscreen.

How had Jack's body lost so many odds and ends? you might ask. Due to some fishing-related accident? Battling the monsters of the sea? Nope... none of the above, he had another job; he was a carpenter, too. A god-awful one at that, and through poor management and disgraceful movements (chopped up by table saws and multiple falls while shingling roofs), he'd ripped and torn himself up a great deal. But the stubborn old mule refused to quit, and he kept up with this trade he had no business being in. His constructions were shoddy and his price unreasonable, but his work ethic was strong, and his rugged manner seemed to inspire confidence among his clients. Fishing was only his hobby—although he seemed well in command of his vessel and unconsciously governed by a natural knack for sailing upon these choppy waters.

26

He must have dozed off because, all of a sudden, he was in a dark void facing a large machine—one that looked like a washer and dryer stacked neatly onto one another, but with humanlike features and many more wires—and there were twelve large tubes plugged into its sides and back and face, all darting out and disappearing into the black abyss at random angles. No. 44 was holding his chainsaw. He started it up and went to work cutting off the large tubes; liquid spewed from these dispatched tentacles as they receded at breakneck speed back into the night. Once he'd cut away all twelve, he sat back—covered in goo—and lit a cigar, content with what he'd accomplished. And then he woke up, and Jack was yelling at him. "The shark, *goddamnit*! The goddamn fucking shark!"

Unbeknownst to him (and still to this day a mystery), Jack had landed himself overboard, still clutching the boat, his other half, drifting from side to side, lay in the jaws of Wayne. Blood shot out and colored the water as he was being chomped in two.

Sometimes we must suffer the injustices of someone else's ideology or essence, fairly or not. And Jack was currently playing victim to the ugly end of that reality—and also to his natural timeline, which was shortly coming to a close, fixated on his violent demise happening in exactly this grotesque manner at precisely this unlucky point. *And how the gods were cruel*, thought No. 44.

No. 44 grabbed his chainsaw and watched Jack go under only to resurface, still half in the jaws of this prehistoric beast, and both man and shark leapt up and onto the side of the boat, unbalancing it, as the shark was now more than halfway beached on their little vessel. No. 44 stared into its eye and lunged his chainsaw at it only to have the shark jerk left at the last moment, releasing the spilled guts of Jack's torso and biting down and ripping off No. 44's left hand as he screamed and bled and tried to work the chainsaw into the shark's side, whirling around in shock. The shark was trying to re-enter the water and disentangle itself from the ship, and No. 44 gathered all the courage he could muster and all the focus he had left, and he plunged the chainsaw into Wayne. The scar-faced shark squirmed chaotically in its death throes that threatened to upend the boat, but No. 44 kept on, cutting away until he'd almost sawed Wayne's head in two.

His shaking right hand picked up his phone, and he tried calling the voice, but there was no reception.

A fishing vessel caught sight of their deranged predicament and picked up No. 44, and they got him to the mainland, and he spent two weeks in a hospital recovering from his wounds. During his stay, he heard no news from the voice and watched loads of daytime television and conversed lightheartedly with the hospital residents and staff. The fisherman came by and brought him an 8x10 photo of the scene he'd stumbled upon. There was great beauty in its composition as the photo had the nearly decapitated shark, Jack's torso, and No. 44 all in a bloody mess, perfectly balanced in the frame with the composition adhering to the golden ratio, and the spiraling of tones and hues (not to mention the stark lighting) giving way to a painterly quality that No. 44 associated with great works of Renaissance art. He asked if he could keep it, and the fisherman said it was a gift.

When he was released, he got a room at a motel, and inspired by a movie he'd watched during his hospital stay (while pumped full of painkillers), he set to work constructing an attachment for his left wrist whose hand he sorely missed. He went out to the hardware store and got supplies and tinkered and toyed for days before he was happy with the results. He fetched the modified chainsaw and fastened it, tightening the screws, and started it up. He gazed at himself in the mirror; a roaring 24-inch chainsaw now replaced the dexterity of his four-fingered left paw, and he cut a table in two, and the limb performed better than he'd expected. He checked himself out in the mirror, and he said, "You talking to me, Bozo?" He motioned upwards with the chainsaw in a mockingly threatening manner and accidentally removed a small chunk from his right shoulder. "Fuck!" he screamed. He turned off the machine and ran to the bathroom and dealt with his newfound gash.

There were still a few kinks that needed to be worked out, but the overall design was quite effective.

27

He was now headed to California—Berkeley, to be exact. *Fuck driving*, he thought. He sold his car and got ripped off by a second-hand car salesman with long, mismatched sideburns, but he didn't care. Money was no longer a concern for No. 44 if it had ever really been; he was, after all, a man of simple tastes. He arrived in California and sent his weaponry via UPS and picked up the parcel at the front office of the Golden Bear Inn near the San Francisco Bay. The tenth victim was a student at Berkeley, and No. 44 was dreading the hunt. He hated universities: the faux grooming of an intellectual elite whose actual mediocrity and uselessness were showing more and more with each passing year. The fall of scholarship and the cancerous echo chamber of bad ideas—thus were No. 44's thoughts regarding the current state of higher education.

He was simultaneously bored and enraged by it.

The day had come, and a rally or march or protest was organized by some angry students; they sighted one of the many world injustices into their crosshairs and decided that by grouping together and yelling about it with likeminded individuals, they could change the world—or break it, or reform it, or loot it, or belong in it. Perhaps one or two even thought they might meet an attractive boy or girl, showing off their ability to care more and *louder* than the rest as a way of wooing their potential mate. No. 44 decided it best to camouflage for the assignment. He went to a low-end but popular retail outlet frequented by teenage girls and picked out a nice dress. A kind young woman helped him out, and he tried it on and was surprised by how comfortable and shapely it was. He went to the drugstore and got some makeup and was rejuvenated by the act of dressing up, and the job was once again fun and exhilarating.

The march was about climate policy and police brutality and underrepresented populations getting a platform and hatred for the patriarchy and systemic racism, and it had very angry young people yelling into megaphones, but the gobbledygook of their jargon was lost in the noise. The lack of cohesion with no definitive (or ascending) icons seemed to be their undoing, or perhaps deep down that was the point. Disorganization and chaos were perhaps part of the seed they were sowing. Disrupt and confuse, even to the point of disrupting and confusing themselves. Good intentions lost in a sea of human toil and conflicting interests. They were beginning to understand that their hopes and dreams were dying and were mostly worthless—and, in the last gasp right before the drop-off towards depression and despondency, they attempted to will the world into the way they wanted it while defying all logic and history that'd come before (2+2=5). They were blind, but what did No. 44 care? It was the way of the youth and would always be so (benign intentions and self-sacrificing sentiments would always be in vogue... and probably ought to be). He just needed to off one of them anyway—a girl named Jennifer Joytown—and according to the database, she'd be at the rally and likely holding a megaphone, one of the elite screamers, the Eye watching and directing bits of the mob's anger towards the precise point or spot or issue they could (and should) be enraged with. No. 44 brought his pistol along with him and had it strapped to his leg beneath his dress. He had a wooden hand fixed to his stump, replacing the chainsaw. Unfortunately, he'd bought the wrong one—a right hand instead of a left one, and the whole thing was ass-backward. *So be it*, he thought. And then he saw her, raised up, standing next to a statue, and he crept up and crouched low and hid behind a garbage bin a few meters to Jennifer's left; he unholstered his gun, and just as she was about to yell, "Fuck the P—" her brains splattered all over the monument and people screamed and chaos ensued and number 10, Jennifer Joytown, was dead (the martyr with a hole in her head).

No. 44 ran easily in his dress; lipstick smeared unevenly on his face. He blended with the crowd. It was a very freeing afternoon.

28

So here we are in our guided hallucination, ninety kills left, and I know what you are thinking. "Wow, Darby, this will take forever. Couldn't we speed this up; hurry this along." And dear reader, you have my sympathies—but, in order for our little spell here to work, we must run along and brave the entirety of the gauntlet. Persevere and triumph through the enigmatic fires of the narrative and hope that when we find ourselves at the end of this adventure, that the time spent accruing the signs and symbols and sensations of our tale add up to an experience that is simultaneously rewarding, worthwhile, and *possibly* enlightening (in one form or another); and you, the reader, can leave having known that you have played no small role here—an accomplice all along, an evil aide dispatching these one hundred souls right along with me. A direct participant, if you will, helping and conjuring the murders and killings stowed away in this here book. For without you, there is no story—it would be the tree in the forest that falls and makes no noise. You are the catalyst, dear reader. So press on, and let your conscience go to bed and let us bathe in bloodlust and bloodshed and ravage in the insanity of it all like an ermine set loose in a henhouse—or maybe it's *not* for you, and you decide to stop. Perhaps, for some, this is it; you've had enough; this is where the game ends, and your journey goes no further. You have taken it as far as you'd like or can. Fair enough, I say. And be that as it may, your humble writer thanks you for your time and sincerely wishes you all the best. But enough of this drivel, for time is a ticking, and many more murders await.

29

He was a divine psychopath settled cozily in the eye of the hurricane, safe and sound from all her silliness and destruction, for she was full of faulty magic and wore a smug and callous smile. Hurricane Maureen made her cut across the Eastern Seaboard of the U.S. of A. as No. 44 returned to the road (having purchased a jeep from a quiet Californian). He was heading down to Mexico. It was time to check out a certain hacienda down there.

30

Crossing the border was a breeze, and it took No. 44 no time at all to locate the adobe farm near Hermosillo. He was going to visit number 11, Juan Gonzalez, and as he neared the hacienda, the final moments of dusk turned towards nightfall, and he saw the bright neon lights stretching out from the backyard of the farm, an extended futuristic glow, giving the whole scene an otherworldly vibe.

He rang the bell, and a woman answered, and she told him to come inside. She said a round was fifty pesos, and he paid at a stall set up in the main foyer without knowing exactly what he was paying for. She led him through the house; it had hand-painted tiles and accents of bashful color. "Come, come, please," she said.

She ushered him through the back door, and he saw an intricately designed mini-golf course elegantly lit. Clown heads and alligators and model castles, not to mention gnomes and fountains, lay bare before No. 44's eyes, and the lady handed him a putter and a purple ball, and then she called out to Juan, and a man in his fifties, gruff and unshaven, popped out from behind an outdoor bar (looking as if he'd just woken up), and he came around and shook No. 44's hand.

"Pleasure to meet you, sir," he said.

No. 44 smiled, and Juan asked if he'd like to play a round together, offer some friendly competition. No. 44 agreed, and the two men set off towards the first hole. They heard a howl, and Juan threw a dismissive hand in its direction as if the coyote or lobo were just another household pet and the hills nothing but the continuation of his massive mini-golf course.

"You go first, señor."

No. 44 set his ball down. The first hole had him facing a small gorge that could only be crossed by a narrow pathway. There was an axe swinging above, a decorative device. He hit the ball, and it tumbled into the gorge.

"Don't worry, sir. Go again; the first shot is always a practice shot," said Juan.

No. 44 tried again, but his luck extended no further than it had the first time. And then Juan set his ball down and aimed his putter. The axe swung indifferently.

They were on the seventeenth hole, and No. 44's game had greatly improved after Juan had a disastrous showing against the clown on the seventh hole whose teeth kept barring his ball from being regurgitating out on the other side. No. 44 watched as Juan's frustration mounted. He smelt sulfur, and he readjusted his fake hand. He wore it retrograde, in a manner that made it look as if his hand was bending backwards or curling in on itself like a dead spider (the right prosthesis in the left wrist). Juan hadn't commented on it, although his eyes had darted towards it earlier as No. 44 set up to make his first few shots.

On the last hole (the nineteenth), No. 44 smacked Juan over the head with his putter. He'd done enough damage to see a small opening in his skull; his brains just poking through. His anger had been awakened on the previous hole as Juan had gotten a hole-in-one and taken the lead. Up until then, No. 44 hadn't even thought about killing Juan (all his focus on sending the ball home), but his frustration with the game, and Juan's arrogant celebration, made him re-embark upon his forgotten quest, and he exerted the full thrust of his force and agitation on Juan's head.

No. 44 hopped the outlying fence and circled around to the front and got into his jeep and drove off beneath the bright and luminous desert moon. "*Another one dissolved to dust,*" sang the radio, and No. 44 lit a cigarette and kept on without turning on his headlights.

31

To hell with it—it was time for a new POV. And Miguel thought that the only way to get home was to drift there, plain and simple. Let the tide guide you back (or take you further and further away). He was investigating the murder of Juan Gonzalez. It was a strange case: a man (gringo), seemingly polite and good-natured, walks into the home/ business of the victim; he purchases a round of mini-golf from the wife/co-owner and plays the entire match with Juan; he then clubs him to death for no apparent reason at the very last hole. *What kind of world was this?* thought Detective Gomez. Although the detective had long ago put to bed the notion that things could ever make sense, this particular case irritated him for reasons he couldn't quite put his finger on; it'd somehow wormed its way past his thick, calloused skin through routes unknown or never before used. Murders, decapitations, dismembered bodies popping up inside rusty oil drums—these were common enough acts, acts that made up a portion of Miguel Gomez's daily life, and he got used to them as detectives generally do—in some ways, he expected them. He had worked the cartels and the slums and the streets and the mobs and had seen the butchery of women at the hands of men, and men at the hands of other men, and children at the hands of other children. He was a hardened soldier fighting against the dark underbelly of human society (in some ways, he too was part of that greater evil, that perpetual darkness, even as he fought to overcome it, to push up against it); his eyes had glimpsed some of the worst acts and impulses his species had to offer. But oddly enough, the scenes that generally stood out to him—the ones that really haunted him—were almost always committed by the supposedly average and everyday citizen; the one who'd run amok, suddenly snapped, right out of the blue—hurtling towards the black. The dentist that goes postal on a Tuesday and rapes his neighbor and stabs his kid.

He'd been eating a hotdog earlier and had a mustard stain on his shirt below the collar that he was unable to hide. He watched as Juan's wife made frequent glances down towards it as he asked her questions concerning her late husband.

When he left the mini-golf course, he already knew that unless he was given (or gifted) a confession or tip or a photograph or video of the perpetrator in the midst of committing the murder, this one, like so many others, would disappear and be forgotten and vengeance and justice for Juan Gonzalez would be nothing but a farfetched dream. *But perhaps that's the way it always is*, thought Miguel. It probably didn't matter much to Juan anyway. If he was dead and enjoying the spoils of heaven or condemned to the fires of hell, he was probably preoccupied wherever he was, and if he was nowhere, well then—all was well. Only his memory could sow havoc, seeking disorder and chaos as it bore into the core of a loved one and tried to turn them from grief-stricken mourner into revenge-seeking vigilante, but such phantoms were generally weak-willed and yellow-bellied and were rarely able to bring this conceit of carnage to fruition. He thought about memories, and he thought about the dead, and then he thought about some old classmates (Roberto & pals); haunted by their youth, Miguel had seen them hanging around the cantinas; they sat drinking, bringing up random and partially fabricated tales from long ago, trivial and uninteresting stories, and they'd yammer on about romances in public libraries, daring feats of mischief and mayhem in the parking lots and football pitches, their first fights and fucks and heartbreaks, amused like pigs in shit, unconcerned that they'd already told the same story twice that night. They lived their lives as if they were on an extended recess waiting for the bell to bring them back to Ms. Fuentes' classroom, towards structure and order guided by her strong and firm matriarchal hand. The nostalgia trap was ruining their lives, or maybe it was what kept them afloat, an inflatable raft of hope and naivety, the last dinghy of illusory promise. Miguel stopped at a restaurant and bought some chips and petted a panting dog hunched over in the shade.

32

She was smoking a cigarette on the balcony of her Parisian apartment located on the fourth floor. She had both her balcony doors wide open, and the wind tossed her hair in gusts, making her appear bombastic and roughed up from the point of view of those walking by on the street. Her dress was blown above her head, and her underwear was clearly visible to anyone who happened to be gazing up at that precise moment; she allowed it to happen, never fighting against it. She looked up and saw her neighbor Jacques and waved; she saw Louise on her balcony, two floors down, and scowled.

She'd been living at the Maribelle Apartment Complex for five years; she was forty-two. She worked long hours at an accounting firm around the corner on rue de Lourmel. She walked to the bathroom and stared at her face in the mirror. When she was a girl, she had suffered through years of horrible teenage acne; big pustules adorned her face and covered her jawline and forehead. The girls at school teased her relentlessly; the boys generally left her alone but not always. She'd tried everything from daily facial cleanses and dietary restrictions to tetracycline, and yet nothing had worked for her. They'd called her Pimply Pam (even though her name was Judy), and she grew up traumatized by the stigma of being unsightly. Years went by, and eventually her face cleared up, and at the age of twenty-two, she sought laser treatment, and from that point on, she was generally deemed pretty and had no shortage of boyfriends and suitors spanning through her twenties and thirties, and she worked out four times a week at home with a large inflatable ball and dumbbells. She was diligent about her Kegel regimen, and she kept a journal and a diary. She was currently seeing a man in his early thirties with a strong oral fixation. He was an engineer. She enjoyed shopping, and she hated dogs. If someone were to ask her where she would rank her life on a scale from 1 to 10, she would give it a solid 7 or a 7.5... depending on the day. She sat down at her dining room table and lit a cigarette as the breeze blew in from the opened doorway of the balcony. Pierre (her boyfriend) was coming by in a few hours. She stared out at the grey-blue sky and listened to the refrigerator as its compressor kicked in.

Judy went out to the grocer's around the corner and picked up some bread and butter and apricot jam. She bought a pork tenderloin and ran into Mr. Dupois, who began to speak in his soft and low and vague manner; Judy edged away and made her way back to her domicile, and when she opened the door, a man with a prosthetic hand was seated on her sofa.

"*Qui es-tu?*"

Pierre greeted the concierge downstairs and made his way up the spiraling staircase towards Judy's apartment. The door was unlocked, and he walked in without knocking. He'd brought along a small gift for her—some chocolates from a newly opened chocolatier near his home in the 14th arrondissement.

"Judy."

No answer. *Odd*, he thought. He set the chocolates down on the kitchen counter and checked the main area and saw her hair draped over the couch as she lay away from him. He tiptoed up to her, believing her to be fast asleep, and when he neared, he realized his error. Her face had a long gash running from her forehead to her chin, pushing everything inward. Her left eye gazed unconcerned towards the window, and her right eye hung limp, dangling from its optical nerve. Pierre stood still and stared, and then he tried to shake her in a lame attempt to wake her or resuscitate her. He did not know CPR—nor would it have helped much at this juncture. He went to the kitchen and phoned the police; he looked at the chocolates on the counter and waited mute.

When questioned by the cops, Pierre was unable to provide any useful clues, and the investigating officers were suspicious of his involvement. *It was always the boyfriend or the jilted lover*, thought Officer Genet. Was it a crime of jealousy and passion? Did she have oodles of other lovers? Had Pierre suddenly flipped (the cold, unfeeling psychopath materializing in her endgame)?

Officer Beatrice scrutinized Pierre as he fumbled with a cigarette and accidentally lit the wrong end.

33

No. 44 felt himself becoming inaccessible and mysterious and wanted. The outside world wanted in, but he had ceased to tolerate its stench. His house was a windowless bunker with a single horribly crooked front door—one would have to chop off their arms and legs in order to enter here, saw down their excess (dispatch flesh and bone) and exist only in their most pure and primitive constituents, a complete submission to reconfiguration, then and only then could they enter. After being broken and hammered again and again by hardships and machetes, only then could they squeeze past. The price was unreachable (and unthinkable) to most, just as he hoped it was. "Fanatics only," read the sign outside the entranceway. The Church of the Few. Fuck compromise.

No one ever knocked, and no one ever entered. He was alone, always. This was just the way it had to be. This could also have been due to the fact that he didn't speak their language (French) very well, and the Parisian way of life was quite unusual for an old brute like No. 44. He sat alone on a terrace full of good-looking people and watched the pigeons shit on statues; he bit into the biscotti and hurt his tooth.

34

Heather was a beautiful Irish girl. She and her pals were drunkenly chanting some polemic song in a jousting and boisterous spirit about the IRA and the Troubles. They were heading towards another pub, singing loudly and carefree, drunk and arm in arm. Emer, another member of the all-girl crew, was checking her phone, currently in talks to rendezvous with a handsome lad later on. She had known the boy for years but had only recently veered their relationship into sexually explicit territory; it'd happened when they'd struck up a conversation by chance at a pub two weeks earlier—and, through the dulling of judgment and inhibitions brought on by drink, they'd ended up in the men's washroom, fornicating in a stall as she bent over the toilet. Mark did not wear a condom, and the next day, as Emer told her story to Heather, Heather laughed and shook her head and asked if she was on the pill; Emer said no.

Emer was scheduled to meet Mark outside McCallund's Pub at 10:30 p.m. She still had time to hang out with her pals, and she and Heather and the rest of the gang chatted and laughed and smoked and guzzled beers and vodkas. At a certain point, Emer went outside to take a call from Mark; the pub was uproarious and loud. But even outside, Mark's slurred speech provided no definitive answer or context as to why he was calling; she couldn't hear him, and she told him to text her, and she hung up. The call had annoyed her, and she thought that maybe she wouldn't fuck him that night. Outside, the streets were empty. Movement and action beyond the immediate vicinity of the pub were nonexistent. She heard the rev of a small motor and saw a shadow leaning up against a brick wall on the other side of the street. Prodded on by drunken curiosity, she walked towards it, and she saw a man standing over an elderly woman, her back pinned against the wall. The sound stopped, and Emer halted her progress. The man turned towards her—his face concealed in the blackness. The drill in his right hand exited the cavity in the woman's head, and he pressed the trigger, and the drill started up again, and bits of blood flew off; he walked towards her, tranquil and slow, as Emer stood rooted to the spot.

35

That night as No. 44 lay in bed, he had an invigorating dream. He dreamt he was about to embark upon a vicious battle. He was living in the 13th century, and he was the leader of some heathen horde, fighting the established order of the day. He held an absurdly large sword in both hands (his left hand was miraculously back in the dream), and he charged in an open field under the darkened grey sky. Mud splattered against his legs as he yelled a hoarse and foul battle cry; his helmet bobbed about as he made his way towards his adversary whose numbers tripled their own. He felt his heart free and content, like a child on its way to an amusement ride. So joyous and carefree, everything felt right even as he hurtled towards his probable end. He was the first to arrive; he swung his sword with all his might and lopped off the head of one enemy, then the arm of another. He ducked and swung and chopped off a leg. He spun and brandished his sword in a three-hundred-and-sixty-degree arc and cut three men open and used his momentum to carry him through towards another powerful attack; he decapitated a horse along with its rider (a general or commanding officer, no doubt), and he continued to hack and slash his way through endless bodies as mutilated corpses piled up in his wake.

He was caked in blood and mud and no longer appeared as a man before his enemy. He had broken their spirit with his sword and his barbarity. His ferocity was heightened by his laughter, which maniacally echoed about as he made his way across the field, delivering his word, his voice, his violence. *What was he?* thought a simple soldier on the opposing side. The battle lasted twenty minutes, and the death toll was nearing a thousand. He had an arrow sticking out of his back, but it only seemed to spur him on. The damage he took invigorated him; nothing seemed to slow him down. A soldier begged for mercy, and he cut off his hands and left him to bleed out. Another spat at him, and he pierced his sword through the man's face and split it in two. At the end of the battle, he took off his helmet and wiped his brow and said aloud, "Today was a good day."

And then he woke up thirsty and crying.

When he got back to sleep, he had another dream, a continuation of the one before. This time he was in a barracks, and a great big muscular man was seated across from him, and No. 44 asked him if he wanted to join his army, and the muscular man said, "Yes, of course." And No. 44 said that he only took the best soldiers, and the man nodded and said he'd killed hundreds of men and feared nothing, and No. 44 smiled. And then No. 44 grabbed an axe and extended his left hand and, with a quick chop, severed it from his very own wrist; No. 44 screamed and passed out, and blood shot everywhere. When he came to, the great big muscular man was seated before him, right where No. 44

had left him; he was as pale as a ghost. And No. 44 handed him the axe, and he said, "Your turn."

The great big muscular man recoiled in fear and said that he couldn't do it; he made up some excuse about needing both hands in order to function at full capacity, in order to be the best warrior he could possibly be; and No. 44 laughed in his face and told him to get out and that there was no place for him here. The great big muscular man walked out ashamed, his head held low, and No. 44 pulled the same trick in the dream countless times (a repetitious gesture) and because it was a dream, each time his hand regenerated, and each time he had to relive the same horrors and atrocious pain—but every now and then, a true one-handed warrior would emerge, and an army was forming. His war chief (or best-in-show) was an eighty-seven-year-old man with no arms who manned a catapult with brutal and dexterous efficiency; sometimes his accuracy could singlehandedly decimate small armies; controlling the whole apparatus with his nimble feet, he controlled the battlefield. The damage he was capable of inflicting was mythic and had exceeded No. 44's own staggering capacity. He was their star player—the old man and his lyre... bashing their brains in and never missing a beat.

He tried to say deep things in trashy ways... or was it trashy things in deep ways?

36

No. 44 was looking through the scope of his rifle. He was on the desert coast of Namibia. The stark contrast between the water and the rolling dunes left him breathless—although, in his brief stay, he'd eaten a fair bit of sand coming up in distasteful gusts of wind, but it was a small price to pay. He'd seen a sign in Windhoek that said, "Inoculate the populace." He wasn't sure what it meant exactly, but he liked it. A truck was coming his way, just as the database had said it would. A man named Silas was supposed to be driving (number 26 on his list), and No. 44 figured he could put a few carefully chosen bullets through Silas from his current spot, and then the truck came into range, and No. 44 pulled the trigger several times.

He spent the rest of the day naked on the beach with no one around, a big smile appearing on his ghastly visage.

37

During his last night in Namibia while out strolling the coastline, he encountered a group of young ruffians dressed in the height of fashion; they accosted him and yelled obscenities his way, and No. 44 was outnumbered and had forgotten all guns and pointy objects back at his hotel. *Shit*, he thought, and then the first blow came his way and then another, and the ebb and flow of body parts caused him to black out, and when he came to, he saw the group walking away. One of the gentlemen had taken his hand (the wooden one), and he seemed proud as a pup with his newly acquired mitt, and No. 44 sat up, and he stared at his vacant stump, and then he ran his tongue around the ridges of his mouth, and he spit out gobs of sand.

38

The voice had organized a covert shipping method (far superior to UPS) which allowed No. 44 to ship his weapons at no charge and almost no risk, with them popping up exactly where they were supposed to be, error-free. *And where were they supposed to be at this very moment?* Australia. Down Under, and No. 44 figured that this constant traveling was really starting to grate on his nerves; he'd been traveling for many moons now, and this constant globe-trotting was getting old. He missed having a main base of operations (even if it was just an old automobile), and he pined for the good ol' days of routine and structure.

After this kill, he'd try and figure something out, negotiate a break, perhaps propose a plan to the voice and see what could be done.

The target was holed up in a motel, and he got a room across from him, and he unpacked his weapons and looked out his window and saw that a party was in full bloom over in the target's room. Earlier in the day, he'd seen the fellow and his cronies by the pool, and their obnoxious and overconfident demeanors had annoyed the hell out of him. They were a youthful bunch of assholes, and No. 44 thought it'd be fun to get his chainsaw out for this one, and he put on an old goalie mask (for theatrical allure) and locked and loaded his chainsaw onto his wrist and grabbed his silenced pistol and tucked two .38s into his pants and strapped a bowie knife around his ankle.

Time to get to work.

39

He kicked open the door and fired at the girl to his left; the chainsaw was at full-tilt boogie in no time, and he cut through a fella from his shoulder to his sternum. He kept firing his pistol, and once it was empty, he observed the scene and noticed that he'd taken four of them out, but the target was still up, and No. 44 dropped the pistol and grabbed a .38 from his pants and fired, walking his way towards his 28th target—his chainsaw erect and coming just in time; he cut through the carbon, the hydrogen, the oxygen, the nitrogen, displaced molecules everywhere. No. 44 looked at the room and himself; he was simultaneously amused and disgusted by his ability to paint a scene in such bold and audacious colors. He walked back to his room, and a bum caught sight of him under the glow of a streetlamp, but he didn't seem to care. A man covered in blood with a chainsaw for a hand was not enough to warrant his prolonged interest. What wonders this man must have seen.

40

He packed up and left in a hurry, knowing it wouldn't be long before the cops arrived. He hauled his weapons out (loaded into a steel crate, behind the motel, ready for pickup) and decided to drive off in his rented van in some direction—still covered in blood, he saw another motel with an easily accessible pool; the clock said 2:17 a.m., and he got out and threw his clothes in a dumpster and lit it on fire; he jumped in the pool, and the blood drifted out and colored the water, and he emerged: naked, reborn, baptized in chlorine. He got back in the van and put on a new pair of undies, and he drove towards a drive-thru and got two double cheese-burgers, fries, a Coke, an apple strudel, and some pancakes with syrup. He'd worked himself into a feeding frenzy; his appetite was insatiable. At the bottom of the take-out bag was a small toy with a pink propeller.

41

He was back in America. Home at last... but for how long? He needed to talk to the voice, figure out a way to stop this constant upheaval that traveling was causing him. For some reason, he felt nervous about confronting the voice. He'd grown fond of it and didn't want to disappoint—and so far, not to toot his own horn, but he knew he'd done a fine job. He was almost a third of the way through the list and was making good progress all the time. But my God, the traveling—it needed to end.

"Hello."

"Yes."

"We need to talk."

"Okay."

"I can't do this traveling much longer. It's really getting to me."

"Okay."

"Okay?"

"Yes, we have something that could work as an alternative

for you."

"Yeah?"

"Yes."

"All right then, what is it?"

The machine was delivered to his new house (151 Cranberry Way, freshly purchased from a blue-eyed realtor), and he placed it in his garage, and it came in a large wooden crate. A big square dropped into the middle of his suburban life, taking up one portion of his two-car garage. He called the voice and asked what exactly the machine was, but the voice wasn't much help; it kept telling him to read the instruction manual that came along with it. "All right," said No. 44, and he tossed his feet up on the sofa and started reading the booklet. The machine was called the Overman. Apparently, the wooden box was actually the machine itself; one side opened up like a door, and he, the operator, was supposed to crawl inside. The outer portion was fitted with a small retractable box (about two inches by two inches). In order for the Overman to function, it needed a token or a guide, a DNA-driven morsel to link it to its destination. The machine was capable of getting inside people's heads, a link to their conscious (or maybe it was their unconscious). A real trippy thing with minimal requirements—slot in a bit of the desired target's hair, blood, saliva, or semen and crawl inside. That was that, said the instructions. Easy peasy Japanesey.

42

There was an alternate name for the machine, too: Job's Dice.

43

He plugged the machine into the wall and figured he'd do a trial run. The voice had sent him a binder filled with bits of hair and saliva, each marked with a number corresponding to the kill list. If the machine worked out, No. 44 could theoretically accomplish his mission from the comfort of his garage if he felt like it. He was still uncertain what the box actually did, and how he was supposed to kill them once he got inside—in their heads or dreams or whatever it was. (Did he just pull the trigger as per usual?) He grabbed a bit of hair from a brush belonging to an ex-girlfriend and put it in the slot and climbed inside the machine.

He felt a breeze pulling him in, and then he felt like he was going down a winding waterslide, speed and blackness—and then *kerplunk*!

A vast metropolis. Skyscrapers and tropical flora, magnificent humidity with a blazing sun. He seemed to be in the business district as everyone was dressed in suits and office attire, and between the glass and steel edifices were sculptural works of art, corporate art, adorning this pseudo-futuristic cityscape. The buildings were massive and silver and blue, and No. 44 took a few minutes to walk around in a stupefied daze, taking in the architecture that was familiar but more advanced and seemed to dismiss certain laws of physics. He looked around and spotted his ex not too far off. She was as beautiful as ever; he'd almost forgotten how lovely she was. He strolled up to her and asked how she was doing. She threw her arms around him and let out an excited screech.

"Jeb! How are you?"

They chatted and caught up, and a giant inflatable cat, like one you'd see at a New York City parade, floated by, and then No. 44 blinked, and they were in an elevator, rising fast. Jump cuts and time cuts—everything reassembled at will. He liked it—he looked down; he was in a suit. He reached into his pocket, and his phone rang.

"Hello."

"What are you doing?" said the voice.

"A trial run."

"Fair enough, but be careful."

Why? What the hell was this? And how in the hell was the voice calling him inside of it, anyway?

"And remember," said the voice. "What you do in there and the amount of time you stay in there have *real* physiological consequences for you, and the same goes for your ex-missus, too. So be careful."

The elevator took them to a suite, and they ate dinner served up by an attentive waiter dressed in a tux. No. 44 bit into a piece of sautéed shrimp, and then he and his ex were making love in a circular bed, and then he told her he had to go, and she said why, and he said, "Because." And she said he was rushing off, just like he used to, right at the precipice, when the iron was hottest, and he said, "Don't be silly," and he kissed her on the cheek, and then a door appeared below a red exit sign, and he went through it, and he tumbled out of the wooden box, and his landing was awkward—practice was needed.

44

The voice finally explained the machine to No. 44, seeing as his glib scan of the instruction manual had only provided the most basic information to him. It told him that anything that happened in there (while inside the Overman) had real physical consequences. It was actually pretty simple, die in the machine, and you die in real life. The most common consequence of dying inside resulted in a stroke, but sometimes, and given enough oomph, the person's head might explode—blood and brains everywhere. Either result was fine, but style points favored the latter.

The voice also reiterated that if he stayed too long, he might get confused and have trouble mapping his way out. Things could get complicated and peculiar in there, just like they could out here. And to remember that any time he wanted out, all he had to do was picture the exit, and a door would appear close by.

45

He put number 32's hair in the machine and let 'er buck. He crawled in, and the familiar waterslide sensation (rushing through the tubes of the universe) was excellent fun for No. 44, and he believed that fun was the sun—an infallible guide. If you were having fun, you were doing all right by most estimations... except, maybe... morally. Those two weren't necessarily mutually exclusive, but they could be.

The scene was strange. He was on the moon or Jupiter or some other rock at a station with concrete monuments and walls—gargantuan and cold and void, and he felt at home. Spacious. He was in a jumpsuit or uniform—as were the rest of the dream inhabitants; it wasn't busy, and he thought it might be a mall, but he could've been projecting. He walked around awhile and enjoyed the sounds and sights of this space oddity out in space.

He saw her passing by a restaurant—but then a large window with an incredible view temporarily distracted No. 44. He seemed to be spinning, rotating along some axis;

stars and rocks moving along some invisible trajectory. It was stirring and hypnotic and made him a bit queasy too. He looked around again for number 32, but she was gone. He kept walking the corridors and nodded politely to the space station's attendants, guests, and workers. Sometimes the people had no face—or their faces were blurred as if they weren't properly created or imagined or integrated, and it was strange, but so was the whole Overman affair, really. The scene shook a little, and then he was sitting down at a food court, and over in the corner was number 32. He imagined a gun under his table, and then he reached underneath, and a gun (similar to his silenced pistol) was taped to its underside. He pulled it out and walked casually up to number 32 and pulled the trigger; the whole scene went crazy—like an earthquake sounding off, and the space station was falling apart, and then he thought about *the exit*, and a door appeared a couple of tables down. He hurried past the scrambling people and jumped through the door, and he tumbled out of the Overman—but he was able to tuck and roll this time in what seemed like a slightly more graceful denouement than he was typically used to.

He called up the voice and gave it his review. He said the Overman was quite a machine—a beaut, really. And then he went for a drive around his neighborhood and stopped off at a donut shop, and he got himself six apple fritters and a coffee, and he went home, and his clock said 11:51 p.m., and he sat on his sofa in the dark thinking of the possibilities and the challenges and the ways he would use the Overman. He licked the glaze from his fingertips and sipped his coffee and stayed up all night watching a horror movie marathon. *Sleepaway Camp, Halloween, Scream.* And he was delighted by his luck, and happiness filled his heart. He woke up late the next morning, sprawled out on the couch. He decided to mow the lawn, and he waved to his neighbor Joe Dunlop who happened to be passing by.

No. 44 checked the internet two days later and searched Cathy Bukowski. He found the Alice Springs resident's obituary; she'd passed away peacefully in her sleep two nights prior. The obituary said she was a loving wife and mother and would be missed by the many people whose lives she had touched. She was fifty-two; she was an elementary school teacher. Cathy's memorial was to be held Friday at the school where she had taught (St. James Elementary School), with all donations going to the local animal shelter.

Her autopsy confirmed that she had died of a stroke.

46

"And remember, you can always kill yourself. Every man is granted that choice. There is always an exit if need be… except if you're stuck in some infinite time loop or some similar narrative trope—or if that goddamn eternal recurrence thing ends up being true. Then we're all fucked—and well… I guess we'll just have to deal with the ridiculousness and maliciousness of it all. Smile at all the crazy. Devour another donut."

No. 44 went back to the donut shop the next evening. These nightly runs were becoming a thing; he was getting fatter, and sometimes he opted for a non-caffeinated tea as opposed to the traditional black coffee… but not always. On this particular occasion, there happened to be a middle-aged asshole with slicked-back hair in a striped polo shirt standing at the counter, chatting on his phone, holding up the goddamn line, and taking his sweet goddamn time; he was really pissing No. 44 off. *Hurry up, you mangy fuck,* thought our hero.

The polo man kept laughing and chatting, a kink in the hose of the donut shop's notorious efficiency, a well-oiled machine that this polo-wearing asshole was grinding to a halt—obstructing the flow. No. 44 glared at him, and the man just stared back, telling him to go fuck himself with his eyes. No. 44 had enough and finally piped up and asked the guy to hurry up. Shit or get off the pot, he said. The man vocalized his own feelings and told No. 44 to fuck off—and even went so far as to make a remark concerning his missing hand, and No. 44 slapped him and pulled out a fistful of hair and left without further ado. He heard the polo-wearing man yell, "I know karate... *voodoo*, too!"

Back at his house, he tossed in some of the polo man's hair into the Overman and crawled inside. The scene brought him to a house on a hilltop. It was night, and he saw some laundry swinging on a clothesline. It was an altogether peaceful scene from the looks of it. Golden hues and tungsten light emanated from the house's interior, and No. 44 saw a fire way off on another hilltop and thought that perhaps some group was gathered there, huddled in its warmth, hiding from the predaceous darkness. He peeked in through a window, and he saw a woman in her late fifties rummaging around, and then he saw the polo-wearing man in a housecoat, but he was *much, much* shorter and *much, much* younger.

He found that bastard snuggled up in bed, believing himself safe from the woes of the world, and No. 44 imagined his chainsaw snug against his wrist, and he disfigured his face, giving it a pterodactyl and conical look. He came in through the window and scared the shit outta that little guy, and the whole fictitious dream-thing started to shake violently, and No. 44 had to concentrate really hard on the exit as the kid's piercing scream shattered windows and walls and even bore into No. 44's head and skull, rattling his brain, and everything was coming down and undone. No. 44 saw the door outside the window and scrambled for it, and just as he was making his way to it—he caught a glimpse of the neighboring hillside on fire, spreading and engulfing the entirety of the slope. No. 44 slammed through the exit door as the ground split beneath his feet.

The next day, he heard on the news that a local resident's head had exploded while walking home. "Just blew right up," is how one eyewitness reported it. People thought he must have been shot (or something), but this was never confirmed nor was it seriously postulated by any of the local news outlets, and when speaking about this strange incident a few days later at the donut shop, No. 44 was asked if people's heads just sometimes explode, and No. 44 said, "Yup... *sometimes* they do."

47

No. 44 was enjoying the Overman. He was able to continue his mission and dispatch the names without ever getting out of his pajamas. Pete Thomsdale, number 34 on the list (the captured gas station attendant), was easily killed one morning, all done in the time it took to make a good cup of coffee; he was thankful he didn't have to backpedal and drive all the way to kill him. His morning routine had him getting up and making coffee, doing some pushups, reading a bit, then heading to the Overman and fetching his daily kill. At this rate, he'd be done the list in the next two months or so. He decided to slow it down a bit and strive for two to three kills a week (sometimes less, sometimes none), with the rest of his time spent reintegrating himself back into the routines of normalcy, the day-to-day grind of modern life. He taught himself how to cook and tried making homemade pasta one night and thought seriously about girlfriends and vacation homes, and he thought it might be time for him to take the plunge, court some young vixen, get back into the game.

Why not?

He downloaded an app on his phone and texted and swiped his way to a date that Friday at an Italian restaurant not far from his house. Wendy was twenty-seven and was the founder of a small niche cosmetics company that prided itself on its ethical conduct.

When he got to the restaurant, he spotted her sitting alone at a table tucked away near the back. She wore a black lace dress with her hair pinned back, and although her online profile might have been a couple of years old, she was still pretty and charming, and No. 44 felt his nerves tingle; the butterflies unleashed from his guts; his penis stiffened.

"Wendy?"

"Jeb! Nice to meet you."

He gave her an awkward hug as she was halfway between standing and sitting; she smiled, revealing her large white teeth, slightly crooked but somehow befitting to the symmetry of her face. She wore glasses that projected a cute and distinguished look.

"How are you?"

Their talk centered on the basics (in the beginning), typical chitchat to get to know the other person—make sure they weren't seated across from some freak or psychopath. They both laughed loudly, and then the conversation turned towards a certain TV personality that they both loathed (prompted by a conversation overheard from an unseen, high-pitched source), and they skewered it with scathing remarks, and they both laughed and found in the other a reflection of their own sick and demented sense of humor.

She came back to his house that night, and No. 44 poured her a glass of wine, and they sat on the couch, and then he kissed her—and when their lips touched, it was strange, a moment of nothing, no spark, just two wet flaps pressed against two others, and then it took hold, and she pulled him in, and he pulled her in, and it was a rush to toss off as much clothing as possible, pull each other together, bring one into the other.

They never made it to the bedroom and fucked on the couch and on the floor, and they used the structure of the sofa as a means to bend and penetrate and mold their way to the other's whims.

When No. 44 got up, Wendy was already gone. She left a note on his kitchen counter thanking him for the evening, and he sat down on the couch and noticed that it had a particular smell to it that morning.

Outside, strolling around, No. 44 saw Joe Dunlop walking his dog, and he stopped to talk briefly with his pear-shaped neighbor. Joe told him that a storm was coming, to expect heavy rains tonight, and to relish in the clean, fresh air that was sure to follow. The dog wagged its tail and made an ill-conceived attempt at a nearby squirrel; Joe tugged at the leash, and the duo moseyed on beneath the elms.

48

No. 44 made himself a fresh cup of coffee and flicked on the TV. He didn't feel like doing much today. If his productivity was measured based on his progression through the list, then he was doing just fine. He was currently at number 43 and decided to take the day off, kick his feet back and have a day to himself. He'd make a nice supper later in the evening and go for a stroll and sit back and see what the television tube had to offer him on this glorious midweek day. He watched as two men competed, running and jumping and climbing, scaling fluorescent obstacles, a time-based challenge with zany commentators and strange cadences. No. 44 grew bored and cruised on to greener pastures. A character said, "Sometimes I need to dream to sleep," and this stood out to No. 44. And then he texted Wendy, but he received no reply. He took a shit and watched a spider spin its web near the ceiling by his showerhead. He farted around like this until supper; he scratched his balls and yawned and wondered if the day was wasted or won.

For supper, he made hamburgers. He sat back on the couch and enjoyed the simple pleasure of a well-cooked meal; he looked down and noticed that the burger's juices had seeped onto his chest and now covered his white shirt with little brown blotches. He scratched his head with his stump and hoped that the universe was conspiring to broadcast another classic film for his enjoyment, but he was denied this pleasure—and then he received a text from Wendy, and she told him that she was seeing someone else. He asked her if it was his stump that'd scared her off; he received no reply. Two days later, he threw away the beef-stained shirt.

49

Over the next couple of days, No. 44 came to a decision; he decided to only have sex with prostitutes (a simplified strategy). He wanted the professional escort with all matters of coitus to be dictated by a dollar sign, a business transaction, no longer a matter of the heart with feelings and uncertainty—he wanted a dependable system: money flopped down and sitting on the counter as the call girl sauntered over and into his bathroom and changed into her bra and panties and then came out to begin the activities requested and agreed upon. She would leave once their time was up, having been handsomely paid (from his POV), and he would have drained his pipes, cleaned his tank—the gun was fired, the cylinder empty—and all would be well in the world again.

He tried this for a month, opting for a whore once or twice a week. This was an agreeable arrangement, the experiment worked, and he kept with the same company but switched around the girls. His favorite, Margaret, was called for multiple times over the month. She was a stunning redhead with a tenacious style and a preference towards more risqué sexual practices. No. 44 favored her among all the others. She was quick to laugh and easy to talk to, and he realized that he was slowly falling into a comfortable and relaxed rhythm with the woman and therefore falling for her; love's spell was working its dirty little charm. *Fuck*, he thought. Could he ever separate his penis from his heart?

He shut down the advances of one girl at the bar during the first week of the experiment; she'd approached him, her eyes glazed, her breath foul, looking for a simple and clumsy night of drunken sex; he kept on with the plan—professionals only. The second woman to approach him (his luck was at an all-time high; his pheromones seemed to be bringing him the damsels in droves, or was it something else?) ended up wooing him with ease, and they had sex in her car, and thus he broke his prior arrangement. He'd paid for her tab at the bar and ordered a round of shots and exhausted the better stores of his charm and energy and charisma. He was worn out by the time they had sex, and his penis had only flown at half-mast during the entirety of the ordeal. In the end, one night with a prostitute had set him back $300, whereas the drunken girl from the bar had cost him $150. But the escort was certainly the professional here, and you get what you pay for.

At home watching the TV on mute, his music blaring, the song said, "Etching icons into the mirror... on the concave glass... waiting on the world to reflect my wrath..." He was watching a nature show on PBS and saw a squirrel up on the screen, and he thought it faggy, and then he saw a whale and thought it niggardly. He fell asleep on the couch with the music blasting in the background, and he dreamt that he was being burned alive the whole night through; he smiled while he slept.

50

(One month earlier...)

He had a surprise coming his way. There was no way of knowing this, but perhaps if he'd paid closer attention, he might have seen the signs, glimmers of what was to be, the fetuses of the future. He'd stopped looking ahead in the list a while back—he was, after all, a lazy son of a bitch, and he simply checked the next target in the database to get a glimpse of their face and features and went to work terminating them based on that alone; he skimmed no further than what was near and next and upcoming. It was really a humdrum affair these days, part of his status quo, although No. 44 did enjoy it—particularly as the Overman had a propensity for creating offbeat worlds or lands for his assassinations to play out in.

No. 44 checked the 44th name on the list and... surprise, surprise: he was supposed to kill himself.

At first puzzled and then slightly intrigued, he slotted some of his hair into the Overman and went to work. *Let's see where this goes,* thought No. 44. *To the world's end or my end or whatever end this adventure ends with, why not take the plunge?*

The Overman took him to a rocky landscape with a seething red sky. Volcanic with infrared textures, he spotted himself in the corner—or what he suspected was himself (the sole creature on this deserted terrain). He noticed that the Overman had a tendency to change the appearance of some of the targets, conjuring them as children or projections or as monsters lurking beneath their shiny, everyday masks. And although this could get confusing, the Overman always seemed to keep the target squarely in the foreground; they were always around, somewhere close by. So long as No. 44 paid close enough attention, he'd find them soon enough. They were the focal point, always near, the center holding together the hallucination.

And there he was. He looked like a flayed man with a goat's head and a long beak. He had no skin, or his skin was reversed or so badly whipped and beaten that blood streaked over the entirety of its surface. Dark red. His face was pulled back, and a hideous smile wore itself on his lips as his permanent modus operandi. He wondered if this was really what he looked like or just the Overman's interpretation of it. No. 44 tried to talk to it, but the beast only howled and lunged when he got too close. He imagined an assault rifle and pulled it out. No suspense would be built, no questions answered, just a swift end for this disgusting and vile creature. Mercy. He pulled the trigger, and its high-pitched wail sent shivers down his spine, and its ribs were split open, and No. 44 imagined the exit, and he headed for the door; and this time, when he came out of the Overman, he landed dolefully and elegantly on his feet.

Well, that was fucked up, thought No. 44, and he walked over to the bathroom and splashed water onto his face. And then he noticed it—a great shock. A goat-headed monstrosity was staring back at him. What the fuck! This couldn't be. But it was. He'd somehow lost his shiny veneer. The mask was gone. Who am I? A goddamn demon from the looks of it. He'd morphed into a rendition of the very thing he'd just killed. He called up the voice and, for the first time, received no answer. What the hell was going on? He scratched at his horns and tongued at his filed-down teeth. *This might take some getting used to*, thought No. 44. "God help me," and then he sat on the couch for a long time, quiet and alone, and then he called the escort service and organized his second rendezvous, and a beautiful redhead walked in two hours later. Her name was Margaret.

51

The month of hookers and horns was a strange one.

52

One thing that stood out to him was that his metamorphosis didn't seem to bother people all that much, neither the whores nor the everyday Joes and Janes. They noticed it, certainly, but people seemed to accept it without much fuss and even seemed to gravitate towards him, more and more in fact, as if his hideous and monstrous look had somehow unearthed a greater honesty that peeled back the layers of grime, an effective cleaning agent, disinfecting some shackle or chain and freeing those clustered in his immediate vicinity. Peeling back the mask as they glimpsed an unfiltered life, the demon life, and No. 44 found that he was overall happy with the changes.

At the end of the month, he stopped sleeping with hookers on such a frequent basis. The experiment was over. He kept them as a reserve option and called from time to time to organize an evening with Margaret or one of the other go-betweens.

53

He slowed his pace again to one kill every week or two. This opened up lots of time for No. 44, and he received no calls from the voice, so he assumed his newfound speed was satisfactory. He walked around town most days, checking out the freshly cut lawns and wandering aimlessly from one neighborhood to the next, confused and overwhelmed by the beauty and mystery hidden in its depths. He was starting to love the place, and it was beginning to feel like home. He hadn't grown up here, but its ability to reinsert itself and untangle his childish enthusiasm, which was really just a way of unmasking the mystery of the mundane, was rich and offered him a new perspective, something different than what he'd grown accustomed to over the last decade or so. He felt in awe of the little things, and with his bloodlust being quenched by the Overman and his weekly or bi-weekly killings, he was becoming an ordinary American citizen once again—a loveable oaf whose appreciation for the smaller bits of Americana (including good apple pie and friendly,

fat strangers and slightly competitive neighbors) had him
waking up content with a smile, a grinning goat face crop-
ping up four to five times a week; the other days, the
melancholic mornings, couldn't be helped, such emotional
heft was buried in his blood. Even at his best, he was still a
sad-sack nihilist at least twice a week. He was who he was.
On those days, it was best he avoided the world and stayed
indoors and masturbated hourly with the drapes pulled tight
and a heaping mound of marijuana a stone's throw away.

54

One night, No. 44 went out walking; he decided to grab a slice of pizza. A fairly good pizzeria stood a mile or so from his house located in a strip mall with a neighboring hardware store, a veterinary clinic, and a convenience store wrapping around its typically vacant parking lot. The owner, a Lebanese man, short and pudgy, not exactly the friendliest at first glance, but over time, through complicated synergy, brow movements, and strategic grunts, had sown an agreeable arrangement with No. 44: the stolid owner and the sinister eater. No. 44 walked in, and the chiming bell of the door announced the scene: a drunken kid, no more than twenty or twenty-one, was arguing with the owner, trying by some inebriated logic to explain the situation to him. No. 44 could see the kill switch turning in the pizza man's gaze (a look he knew all too well). The drunken kid was cursing the owner, saying that he'd insulted him, shit on his honor, so to speak—and the owner was doing his best to get the kid to leave, to no avail. No. 44 watched patiently, and then he saw the kid go for the jugular—he yelled, "Well, fuck your wife... I'm gonna fuck your wife... I'm gonna fuck *your* fuckin' bitch real good." He laughed as he said this (a maniacal hyena), and No. 44 watched as the owner—with angry, bamboozled brows—grabbed a knife and came around the counter.

The first stab didn't seem to register. Blood shot out from the kid's neck, and his eyes only understood when the knife slid back in again. He slumped over in a pool of his own blood—the shock fading from his face with the last kick of life—his head flapping back like a Pez dispenser. The owner looked at No. 44, his expression mute, the knife still in his hand, blood all over his apron, and No. 44 asked for two slices of pepperoni... *please.*

The pizza man had given him a whole pizza free of charge, and No. 44 stepped out without inquiring about the dead boy or the incident. He felt that by accepting the pizza, he had somehow signed a pact with the pizza man and pledged his silence in the ordeal. He walked home munching on the chow and wondering what movie he felt like watching that night.

55

No. 44 woke up the next day feeling good. He went about his typical routine, and this not being a kill day, he decided to go for a long walk in order to burn off some of the excess calories that'd accrued from the night before. He thought about happiness, and the happiness he felt, and why now, at his most routinized, did he feel the closest he had in a long time to describing himself as happy. He wondered about this feeling; a sense of ease was probably the best way of describing it. The word itself, *happy*, was strange to him, foreign in lots of ways. He had forgotten the calm enjoyment one might feel wading in warm waters (cannonballing into the deep end of the neighborhood pool), the beauty of a sunny afternoon after a midmorning downpour, the drift and power of momentarily letting go—of having a coffee in the backyard (the lush green grass...) while eyeing the neighbor's tomato plants. It felt good to reconnect to this calm; it provided a fresh coat of paint. Happiness was all about the eyes, *los ojos*, thought No. 44. Perceptions and interpretations were the founding principles of someone's mental fortitude, and without a solid base watching and configuring and discarding the information beaming inward (structuring it to the ingrained astigmatism of the host's vision), No. 44 felt that a good life was probably out of the question. He watched a dog piss on a tree and an older woman struggle past, eyes directed downward, scowl on her chubby face. He bought a pack of gum at a convenience store and continued his stroll. He walked past the pizzeria from the night before, busier than ever, the murder nothing but a minor hiccup in an otherwise perfectly flowing system. He felt like smoking a joint and did so. He sat on a bench and drifted into a daze. He dreamt of predatory birds.

He woke up on the bench, and his head felt heavy; tilted backwards, gazing up at the sun, he rubbed his neck and noticed a beaklike protrusion emanating from his face. What the hell? Another metamorphosis? *Goddamnit*, thought No. 44. Could the gods be so cruel? And the answer was yes. And now he had a beak to back up his horns and his once goat-like face—which was stranger than ever, transformed yet again; it bore the shape of a triangle, conical, arched out and elongated: a beak with a cornucopia of odd outgrowths and black beady eyes. He took out his phone and snapped a photo of himself and was once again appalled by the result. One could only hope that the changes had reached their climactic end. He was the apotheosis of obscene. He could no longer describe himself as pretty.

When he woke up in the morning after a long night tossing and turning, unable to sleep—in utter disarray during the hour of the tiger (3–5 a.m.)—he noticed a weight to his limbs, everything was heavy. He heaved himself out of bed and went to unload his bladder. His eyes were opening, the crust cracking, and he saw gargantuan toenails protruding from gargantuan, scaly feet. *Again*? And so it was, new feet (claws included!) and a new hand with fingers sharper than scissors. He tongued around in his mouth and noticed the increased length of his lingua and felt around and opened up his jaw in front of the mirror; he found a prehistoric concave mass of gnarled fangs crammed inside, ready to chomp down on anything resembling food. He looked down and even saw the budding nub of a new left hand in the infancy of its growth. At least, he thought, he could jerk off left-handed again—so long as he minded the blades, and then his heart skipped a beat, and he took a good look at his pecker, and my gosh... "from tip to top and shaft to base," he was a man reborn, a devil with a mean ole dick.

56

He called up the voice that morning. He figured that the voice would know what was going on—hell, it could have even planned this for all he knew... or at least foreseen it.

Ring, ring.

"Yes?"

"What the hell is going on? What the hell am I turning into?"

"Hmm, have there been changes?"

"Yes!"

"Send me a photo."

He did so, and the voice waited a long while before responding.

"This isn't uncommon, especially due to the nature of the task and the duration of its ascent. I hope you still plan on continuing."

No. 44 let out a groan, signifying that he was still up to the task. In reality, it was one of the things he looked forward to most, especially as he'd slowed the list over the last while. He was currently at number 53, nudging past the halfway mark two weeks ago. He hung up and showered and got dressed and went out for another stroll. A three-legged bullmastiff was wandering around the street, dragging a leash behind its muscular neck; it hobbled along. No. 44 stood and watched the dog as it came his way. He put out his hand, and the dog sniffed it and then licked it, and No. 44 sat down on the curb, and the dog followed suit. He petted the beast (being careful with his new fucked-up fingers) and sat mumbling to it for ten minutes. A few people passed them by, but no one took ownership of the dog, and No. 44 got sick and tired of waiting and took up the leash himself, and he and the dog walked on. He felt good having a partner to stroll around with, two queer-looking beasts trudging along on the sidewalk. He waved to Joe Dunlop and his dog, and Joe waved back and said nice dog. No. 44 smiled and kept on with his new companion. He walked over to the convenience store and bought some water and a Tupperware container and some beef jerky and poured the dog a drink and shared the beef as they sat beneath the sun.

They walked back, taking the same old route, slow and steady with his three-legged friend. And then No. 44 saw a woman—down the way—in cutoff denim shorts, looking frantic, and when he caught her eye, she came running over, tossing her arms around the dog. Master and mutt reconnected.

"Betsy! Where have you been?"

"I found her wandering around. Nice dog you got here, ma'am."

They chatted for a bit; the young missus, so thankful for having retrieved her dog, gave No. 44 her number and wandered off with Betsy. She glanced back at him as she walked away and smiled, and No. 44 looked down and noticed that his left hand had grown. That night, he dreamt that someone had stolen one of his ribs.

57

An alligator in his backyard! That's what No. 44 woke up to this morning. A curious sight. Its long reptilian frame right out in the open, still and prehistoric—he stood on his deck and watched it lie among his grass. Its eyes—mutant, primordial oracles of base desires. He opened his fridge and found some raw chicken and took it outside and tossed it to the reptile. It moved fast, and the agility of its tiny legs made No. 44 giggle. In some ways, he found the alligator a fitting backyard companion. Sure, it wasn't as lovable and playful as the three-legged dog from yesterday, but it had its charms. He unfolded a lawn chair and sat outside and watched the alligator. *How the hell had it gotten in here?*

He'd fallen asleep, and when he jolted awake, the alligator was gone. He walked around the boundary of his fenced yard and saw no points of access or entry and thought the alligator must be a cunning little son of a gun. He folded up his chair and went back inside. He went through his binder and found number 53's hair and went to the Overman.

Number 53 on the list was Devon Plymouth, a ginger fella who appeared to be in his early forties. No. 44 had learned that the Overman functioned differently when compared with reality in how it viewed his devilish new guise. The stark contrast between the outside world, which typically accepted (or ignored) his fucked-up physique, and the Overman, that often colored him as a revolting and frightening sideshow creature, was an odd dichotomy—although the Overman was only partly to blame. Indeed, he was very much taking advantage of his *new* look while inside the machine, the conductor carefully orchestrating the scenes in order to get the desired effect, the most from his get-up, tweaking the lighting and the sound, the temperature and the mise-en-scène, often to achieve peak terror—he very rarely needed to use weapons anymore. A good scare, preceded by some carefully scripted stalking, usually filled the target with enough fear that they erupted… blowing their top. He was a crafter of tones and atmosphere in the Overman, ramping up the dread until the boiling point was reached and his next victim popped. An auteur of the macabre, a killer craftsman.

He saw Devon in the corner sitting by a Christmas tree. It was well past midnight, and he was alone in his pajamas, an excited ten-year-old, and No. 44 imagined a big gift, and he set himself inside of it, folded up like a skin suit (preparing to be reinflated… reanimated), compact and ready to pounce. He added tufts of orange hair and a circular nose and purple eye shadow to his dehydrated face.

Devon went to work and unwrapped the gift, and the moment No. 44 rose out, Devon froze and gripped his chest, and No. 44 opened his mouth, and the clown bit down and off went Devon's head.

When he got out of the Overman, he thought to himself that he felt better, but for some reason, his mind said "badder," and when he went inside to take a shower, he noticed tiny protrusions coming out from his back. What the H were these? *Wings*? And then he heard someone on the radio say, *"Don't strive to be good; strive to be effective."*

58

Do all alligators go to hell? And was morality simply the shifting tide of social norms governed by guilt? Musical chairs to reduce the nonconformists, one round at a time?

59

Two weeks had gone by, and by then, No. 44's small bony back masses had blossomed into enormous wings with incredible width. He estimated his wingspan to be roughly three meters long. He felt like a dog with two tails, and it took him some time to adjust and coordinate. He'd attempted to wear a T-shirt, cutting out a portion from the back to make way for his wings, but this proved to be a disaster, and he let the idea go shortly after his first attempt. He would toss on shorts, but he no longer had any use for his shirts or shoes. He had great difficulty getting into his vehicle (although he was able to *just* squeeze in, given he folded his wings in just such a way), and so he adopted walking as his main mode of transportation. He figured he'd need to reorganize his life now that he was no longer of a compact or typically human variety.

There was a park not far from his house that belonged to two neighboring schools. One Saturday, No. 44 walked over there and ambled up a small hill bordering the two institutions and stood at the top: he was there to see if his wings held any purpose beyond the decorative. He'd tried before to thrash them into flight, but he'd only succeeded in becoming airborne for a brief moment. He ran down the hill at full speed and started flapping away as best he could—but nothing happened; he kept at it though, and forty or so minutes into his downhill sprints, he felt his feet leave the ground and his large scaly wings thrust him upward; he got a good fifty feet into the air, riding the currents, and he did a loop around the schools' perimeters and landed safely back where he'd started; his heart beat fast from the excitement of his first completed flight. No. 44 was surprised by his ability to man this new hardware rather effectively (once he'd grasped the basics, of course). He wondered about his endurance... *about how high he could fly*. Over the next week, he tried farther and farther voyages, going higher and higher, and he noticed that neither the thinning air nor the temperature nor the gusty winds held him back. He was impervious to the assault of the elements, and he spent much of his time out in the open skies, not tiring in the slightest, circling with the birds and munching away on the odd protein-rich seagull. He figured he could get used to the high-flying life.

60

"*Horror is a well-built feeding trough,*" he felt, and if nothing else, he felt he was at least a fairly interesting hunk of meat, or so he thought, and he decided to call Abigail—the girl with the three-legged dog. He set up a date, and she promised to bring Betsy, and three days later, she rang the bell, and No. 44 opened up, and she kissed him on the cheek, and he petted the dog, and he invited them in.

He set out a bowl of water for Betsy and got beers for Abigail and himself. She—the dental hygienist—had moved to town two years prior. It was a little over a year since she'd found Betsy at the pound ("her sad canine eyes")—and it'd taken one sleepless night and an intense argument with an ex-boyfriend before she'd been allowed to take the dog home. After two beers (and some trifling exposition), the trio went for a walk; the sun began its slow descent, casting elongated shadows while exhibiting its array of fantastical hues; soon it would settle into the totality of darkness, another day gone. They arrived back at the house, and No. 44 asked Abigail if she'd like to go for a flight, and she said why not. They left Betsy to her own devices; they made for the skies, and No. 44 scooped Abigail up, and off they went, whizzing and shooting through the air, an acrobatic feat with romantic connotations.

When they got back, they noticed a whining sound. They saw smears of blood, a trail leading across the kitchen and 'round the counter, and No. 44 peeked, and he saw Betsy sprawled out, another leg missing, down to a duo, a whimpering canine bleeding out. Abigail screamed, and No. 44 saw more blood leading to the back door (slightly ajar); he caught sight of the alligator back there, blood on its snout, chewing vigorously. No. 44 ran after it, shooing it away, and it ducked nimbly under a narrow portion of fence obscured by long grass. When he got back inside, Abigail was on her knees, tears streaming down her face, gripping her dying dog. No. 44 didn't say much; he picked up Betsy and went outside and batted his wings, and off they went.

He flew towards the veterinary clinic near the pizzeria.

The clinic was open, and Dr. Voss sedated Betsy and went to work on the dog. No. 44 sat outside on the curb, covered in blood. He was hungry and grabbed a slice of pizza from the pizzeria next door; he nodded to the pizza man as he entered the restaurant, and the pizza man asked no questions.

Abigail stayed at his house that night; they slept in the same bed; she could barely sleep, and he lay snoring, dreaming of his father. And in the dream, he was showing him a painting he'd done, and his father smiled and said, "Good work, Son." But the old man was lying, and the boy knew it, and the boy said, "Father, I know you're lying. Tell me the truth." And the old man's smile widened.

He told the boy that it wasn't good, and he said that in order to be good, he would have to mutilate his body and dissect his soul, that was *the way...* the only way, for no other way was open to him—and not only that, but he must hide his wounds and these operations so that no one could see them, and if this required him to shun the world (and be alone), so be it. He should continue to reconfigure himself until only his essential elements remained. And during all this, he should keep his injuries hidden. He will be deemed mediocre, and all his pain and suffering will never see the light of day: pity will be unknown to him. He will keep it inside and cultivate it, tend to it, and wait patiently for it to blossom. "That's the path, Son... and when the horror stories become nothing more than romantic comedies, you will know the end is nigh."

And when No. 44 woke up, he thought that most of his defeats had been small and humiliating affairs. He figured he wasn't alone in this.

61

No. 44 took Abigail to the clinic the next morning, and she was told that Betsy would recover. She would have to use a wheelchair for hind-leg support from now on, but the dog would live.

No. 44 left Abigail at the clinic and went home to plot his revenge against the alligator.

He set out a mound of meat in the middle of his yard, anticipating that the alligator would return especially now that it'd got a taste for his well-stocked home. He put his lawn chair out on the deck and made himself a cup of coffee and waited patiently for the reptile to arrive. A shooting star shot across the sky, and he looked at the five homemade bolitos sitting next to him.

Bolito: a contraption made up of an alloy steel cable tie with a small motor attached. When activated, it would tighten until its noose became a knot, nearly impossible to cut, and when wrapped and triggered around a neck or an arm, it would most certainly cut through it with the ease of a hot knife slicing through butter.

The sun had long ago set, and the alligator had yet to appear, but No. 44 sat patiently. He was a good hunter and knew how to wait. He thought about his life, little moments from his youth, biking along the canals of his hometown, stopping at the diner for a hamburger and a milkshake; he watched as his memories provided ample fodder to get him through what some might have called "dead time." (He thought of a goth girl dancing on the roof of a blue sedan at his first teenage party...) He knew boredom, like everyone else, but he also knew the beauty of quiet contemplation and lonely, wasteful afternoons. Wisdom and age had graced him with the gratitude to appreciate these silent moments peppered here and there; whether he was sitting alone waiting to be called for a hair appointment or twiddling his thumbs on a lawn chair waiting on an alligator, he did not think of these times as squandered, although they might have been. His phone rang, and Abigail told him that Betsy was improving. She thanked him for his help, and she hung up without saying goodbye. He looked up at the moonless sky and fiddled around with the bolitos.

62

He heard a scurrying in the corner and saw a snout poke its way through the grass. It eyed him as it approached, and No. 44 sat still, not moving a muscle. The alligator neared, easing its way towards the feed, and No. 44 remained cool and calm. It took a bite and started to eat, and it pulled some of the meat towards its exit. No. 44 waited until it took another large mouthful, and then he pounced and jumped on it. It tried to run, but his weight and his heft were too much for it, and he dragged it across the grass and attached a bolito to each of its legs and then around its tail, and he let the beast go. It only got a few paces before it seized up. Its hindquarters were the first to burst, and No. 44 watched as each leg was severed, leaving behind a defeated torso without a tail. He lifted up the body and the head; it oozed blood, and its snout made slow minuscule movements up and down. He looked into its eye and then tossed it back on the grass and went and collected the rest of it.

63

He prepared the alligator that night and decided to use some of it for a stew. He froze most of the meat, saving it for another time. He put the head in the freezer, and when he tasted his concoction, he felt that the meat had a mild flavor to it, landing somewhere between chicken and fish.

A month or so later, No. 44 had Abigail and Betsy over for dinner. He served up another batch of his alligator stew and presented Betsy with some seared meat from the alligator's tail. Neither Betsy nor Abigail was overly thrilled with the meal and each seemed to shrug off the victorious rite of eating their fallen enemy. When they left, No. 44 was annoyed; after all, he'd done most of the butchery for their benefit. He watched the dog through the window and felt sorry for it with its contraption of wheels hoisting up its rear haunches, a parody of the mobile beast's golden days—although, to be fair, the dog seemed to be indifferent to its altered state, going from three legs to two, a negligible change to the animal's jovial disposition. He went down to his freezer and got out the alligator head. He looked closely into its eyes and felt the strange sting of comradery. The next day, he took it to a taxidermist and got it mounted; beneath the head, he had the word "friendo" inscribed.

He placed the alligator head on his living room wall and routinely gazed up at it.

64

"At a certain point, all that matters is style."

He is driving through the desert. Cars zoom by along an unknown secondary highway, and No. 44 spots Dylan James two cars ahead. He flashes his blinker and passes the car in front of him, veering into oncoming traffic, smashing down on the accelerator; the wind whips at his face, and the convertible picks up speed as a pack of vultures nip at the spine of some indistinguishable roadkill a few yards back. He blasts the radio; it is competing with the sounds of the road: asphalt and wind and the worn belts of an overheated motor. He sips the beverage he found in the cup holder next to him; he can taste the sharp notes of whiskey cutting through the stale, day-old coffee. Dylan is just ahead. He grips the steering wheel with his claws and decides to play deconstruction derby out here on the open roadways; he rear-ends Dylan, who cocks his head back and then speeds up. No. 44 laughs and thinks that he's got himself a chase.

He looks in his rearview mirror, and the road looks like a fucked-up face. A really fucked-up face, he thinks.

Yippee-ki-yay!

He bashes into the side of Dylan's car and sends him into a tailspin and then a rollover, and the scene begins to shake, and he envisions an exit, and he jumps out of his car like a crazed adrenaline-fueled ballerina and spirals through the air towards the exit at speeds topping 100 mph. He gets a glimpse of Dylan whose body is merged with the inanimate components of the vehicle: the machinations of death have claimed another victim, and then he's out of the Overman and back in his garage, and something grazes his ankle, and he notes that the final piece of the puzzle has clicked into place just above his ass, and he wags his newfound tail that has a spade-like shape at its end. He slashes it around and stabs at the air and wags it like a good dog.

65

That night, he dreamt that he was beaten within an inch of his life, blood and wounds, charred lips with burns, gouges ejected from his physique. A mound of meat in his own right, ready to keel over and dwell in the earth—*food for worms, lads, food for worms.*

Betsy was in his dream too, and she wandered over through the mist and sat beside him, comforting him, licking his wounds, and then he woke up... and everything was different. He was on a cot and weighed approximately one hundred and ten pounds, an emaciated mess of a man in a fifty-square-foot cell. A poster on the wall said, "Welcome, Bandito." He got out of bed, his joints stiff with pain, muscles atrophied from lack of use. No longer a scaly monstrosity of strength and virility, but a weakling of jaundiced flesh with years of beard growth and insanity rotting away in his brain. The steel door barring his way had a small opening in it; he yelled, "Hello," but received no reply. He took a dump in the toilet and tried to wash his hands in the sink; it spit brown water his way, and he sat on the edge of the bed and stared at the muted yellow walls. The corner of the ceiling was leaking.

66

A guard came by and opened his cell door. He yelled: "On your feet, prisoner. Prepare to be counted!" No. 44 walked out of his cell and got a glimpse of the other inmates for the first time. He cocked his head to the left and to the right, large and small men of varying colors all staring straight ahead except for No. 44 who had loads of questions concerning his whereabouts and who he was.

Once he'd been counted, he was ordered back into his cell; a tray of breakfast was delivered through a slot near the bottom of the door, consisting of spoiled milk and a few flakes of cereal tossed into the fold. A sludge resembling coffee accompanied the dish, and No. 44 wondered how he'd gotten himself into this mess. He envisioned an exit, but none appeared. He stared at the leaking roof, and then he tried to bang out some pushups. He was able to do four before his arms gave out.

His cell consisted of a small cot, a sink, a toilet, and a poster. There was a small shelf on the wall with a few books lying on it. The rest was bare. The floor was concrete. There was a small window, and if he pulled his bed over and stood on his tippy-toes, he could almost glimpse a far-off horizon. The only sounds he heard were intermittent screams reverberating from some unknown quarter, zigzagging through the corridors until it arrived at his flea-bitten ears.

During the next morning's counting, he asked the guard where he was, and the guard struck him with his nightstick. His reply was violence, and No. 44 understood the rules then, and the next day, he collapsed under the weight of three pushups.

That night, he dreamt of his grandfather. He was just a boy in the dream, and they were taking a trip through the Rocky Mountains and were driving along in an RV, and No. 44 and his grandfather chatted as the old man drove, and they listened to music and took in the sights of giants rising before their eyes. Flat prairies made way for a sudden shift, a showcase of immense stone, spatial vertigo caused by the uproarious presence of stature and strength and fortitude. Bugs splattered against the windshield, and the blue-striped dragonflies displayed their inner mush on the glass canvas. His grandfather smiled at him, and No. 44 flipped himself upside down on the passenger seat and watched the inverted masses pass him by.

"Sometimes, the only way over is through," said his grandfather. "And sometimes, God hides in the soap."

67

The next morning, he was taken out to the courtyard with the other prisoners from his wing. They walked in the same counterclockwise loop over and over again. Some men smoked and talked, but most were silent. No one spoke to No. 44, and he looked up at the guards in their towers with their automatic weapons. The fences were coiled with barbwire, and No. 44 watched one man—slightly taller than him, with a patchy, ill-formed beard—cry silently as he walked in continuous circles around the yard with the others. He was the only one displaying anything other than despondency or disgust or concrete stoicism on his face.

When No. 44 returned to his cell, he noticed that his poster had been changed. It said, "What now?" and had a picture of a duck comically folding its wings, personifying the quote in an awkward stance that quite possibly would've made No. 44 laugh had it not been for the strange details surrounding the poster's sudden appearance. He guessed that a guard might have changed it, but this rationalization seemed absurd. The nightstick-brandishing guard occupying himself with decor? His supper slipped through the gate and cut off his train of thought; he snatched it up as fast as he could. From what he could tell, it was a stew, grey in color and chock-full of some mysterious meat. It tasted better than he'd expected, but his hunger was insatiable, and the small portion didn't make a dent, and he groaned in his cell and chewed on a ripped piece of bedsheet, gnawing it into a pulpy mass before allowing it to descend into his guts.

The next day, he remained in his cell. He stared at the poster and peered at the sky through his small window. He used the spoon that came with his lunch to make up a beat and summon a rhythm. He tried to do five pushups but only got four. A bird perched on his windowsill; it was the best part of his day. There was one light in his room, and it colored everything in a faint yellow-orange glow; a black smudge impaired part of the bulb and obscured some of the light. He had no control over the illumination; it turned on every evening around dinnertime and went out at some point an hour or two after sundown.

He was walking in the courtyard, doing his loops, when someone tapped him on the shoulder. He turned and saw a man, short and bald with large popping eyes.

"How'd you get here?" asked the bald man.

"Don't know."

"Did you just wake up here one morning, and *boom*, you was in a cell?"

The question seemed strange, possibly because the man had insinuated that waking up here without a clue was a common enough occurrence to warrant the query.

"I just woke up here."

"Same. I wonder why that is. Ah well, the mysteries of confinement, I suppose."

He walked away and joined another section of the loop; he smiled and gave No. 44 a hearty wave.

During their next stroll two days later, No. 44 watched as the blithesome prisoner he'd spoken with was stalked and preyed upon. A bearded man with a solemn and aggressive stride sped up, taking the outer lane and passing the corralled convicts; his eyes fixated on the congenial man from yesterday's yesterday. When he caught up to him, he pulled a shiv and stabbed him in a series of quick and decisive jabs. The guards fired their guns, and two inmates, including the perpetrator and another prisoner (who happened to be in the wrong place at the wrong time), were gunned down.

The next day, No. 44 was escorted to the shower house. It was a long hall with showerheads dropping from the ceiling, uncoiled and slinking down, controlled by some out-of-sight master switch. As he stood naked and shaking with the other prisoners from his wing, water poured out, first scalding hot and then ice cold. He shivered as he was marched back to his cell; he chewed on more of his bedsheet and started to cry. He missed naked women and alligator heads. He looked near his bed and saw "God only speaks in stylized blurbs" etched into the wall.

68

He dreamt of himself that night—but himself in his former state as the horned demon with the strange beak and the bulky build with the great menacing wings and the sharp, agile tail and the devil dick. He was there too in his current emaciated state (the POV from which the dream was viewed), and the demon was talking to him, outlining a plan. It told him that danger was lurking, and tomorrow someone was coming for him, someone with violent and deadly intentions. He should shout the word "Soap" when this individual approached. No. 44 tried to talk to his former self, but he flew away, flapping his great wings, off into the blinding light of God-knows-where.

When No. 44 woke up, he felt strange and weaker than usual. His arms were heavy. He ate breakfast and stared at the wall and waited for the walk that never came. And then his cell door opened, and no one was there. He stepped out and looked to his left and to his right, nobody. *Weird*, thought No. 44, and he waited, figuring that if he went out strolling around on his own, he'd probably be shot or knifed or beaten or reformed and repackaged as a bloody and broken mess. He heard footsteps coming his way, clanking on the metallic floor. He saw a man, another prisoner, far-off, walking quickly with purpose in his direction. He seemed to be gripping something, and No. 44 thought back to the scene in the yard with the shiv and the friendly fella and the shooting and the deaths. *This son of a bitch is coming to kill me,* thought No. 44. He hurriedly looked through his cell for a weapon; he couldn't find anything better than a hardcover book. The footsteps were nearing, louder and louder; the man was almost there, and No. 44 backed against the far wall and readied himself; he waited for what was coming. The man rounded the corner, waving his knife, and No. 44 instinctively yelled, "Soap!" And the man stopped dead, and then the crazed look in his eye dissolved as if all the energy had been sucked out of him. He was deflated and stood still and readapted to the mood of the scene; he had a tattoo on his face, and No. 44 saw that the knife was a rounded piece of glass, resembling, as far as he could tell, a grizzled talon.

"Tomorrow," said the man.

He walked away, leaving No. 44 alone in his cell. The door swung closed of its own volition, and he heard the lock jam into place.

He didn't sleep a wink that night.

A guard came and got him in the morning; he didn't say anything and escorted No. 44 out to the yard. The man who'd come by his cell (brandishing knife and hostility) was out there along with three other guards. One guard said, "Gentlemen, you know the rules. One shot each per turn until we have a victor. We'll flip to see who goes first."

His adversary called heads, and the coin landed on tails, and they handed No. 44 a .44 Magnum loaded with a single bullet. *What the hell was going on?* They positioned him and his attacker roughly thirty feet apart, and a guard said, "Take aim!"

No. 44 fell into a brief hallucinatory state at this point and saw his old winged self appear in his mind's eye. It told him *not* to fire at his opponent, to purposefully miss, fire at the ground. "Don't try," said his deviled self, "that's the key."

No. 44 did as he was told and fired at the ground. The guards booed him, and his opponent wasn't sure how to react. He could have taken this withdrawal as an act of kindness or friendship or generosity, but he did not. It infuriated him. Why was this punk not playing by the rules? Didn't he know how Soap worked? Does he think he's tougher (or meaner or better) than me? Who's he to rain mercy down on the likes of me? *I'll show him*, thought the crazed tattoo-faced duelist, and he raised his gun and placed the barrel against his head, called No. 44 a coward, and pulled the trigger and blew apart his head.

A strange victory, to be sure, and when No. 44 was out walking, doing his loops later in the week, a nearby inmate informed him that the man he'd killed (Francis DeBlussy) was one of the most feared and dominant prisoners in the whole block. No. 44 was making a name for himself as an unorthodox captive with an indirect style of murder. "Nice," said No. 44.

69

The guard asked No. 44 what heaven was like. This seemed like a strange thing to be asking a prisoner. Was this a trick? The guard had come to his cell and spoken those exact words: "*What's heaven like?*" ... How would No. 44 know? But he knew he should come up with an answer or risk another beating, so he said that it was exactly like it was here except everything was inverted. "Heaven is the inverse image of this image, its holy reflection."

"So, in heaven," said the guard, "left becomes right, and right becomes left? I'm in there... and you're out here?"

The days kept on, and because of the death of the self-sabotaging duelist DeBlussy, No. 44's clout among the prisoners had risen substantially. Rumors and lies were interwoven and working in his favor, promoting him as a paragon of violence and power and recklessness—a Machiavelli of the prison yard, capable of deluding the most hardened criminal minds into self-destruction; he was a skinny mess of a thing with a serpent's tongue, beyond the vulgarity of a good shiv. The guards brought him better food, and prisoners he didn't know nodded to him. He did six pushups, and sweat trickled down his cheek.

70

He had another dream in which his former winged self appeared and told him that he'd just killed number 58 on the list, Francis DeBlussy. Number 59 was a guard named Jordan Everstein; he'd meet him in two days' time. Be patient, said the beast, you're doing great.

In the morning, he received a cinnamon bun and an espresso for breakfast. He ate and did seven pushups and read some of the Bible and thought about the joys of incarceration. He was popular here, or perhaps he was feared, and maybe even respected. Whichever way, he was acclimating to his surroundings and enjoying the harsh routine. He missed the Overman, but his dreams had reinvented themselves in here and turned up the volume as if to keep his invigorating imaginings in peak form.

When he was being counted later in the week, he saw a new guard and wondered about him and thought he might be Jordan Everstein. He asked another guard he'd acquainted himself with if Jordan Everstein was in today, and the guard nodded and pointed over to the fella No. 44 had earlier seen, the "new" one—but how would he kill him, and more importantly, how would he kill him and get away with it? What schemes could his nefarious mind draw up? He sat in his cell, mumbling to himself and waiting patiently for his brain to unlock the proper code and pour forth the secret elixir of how to butcher a prison guard in prison and get away scot-free.

Once again, like a cheat code falling from the heavens, his guardian angel (his former meaty self) appeared in another dream and drummed up a plan. He listened attentively; he glanced around, a train station, "Platform Nine and Who the Fuck Cares...", and No. 44 watched as a young mother bid her daughter farewell. They embraced one final time before the young girl boarded her ride. And as the train pulled away, the young girl stuck out her head from the window, and she waved to her mother whose face, when No. 44 looked closely, appeared both reptilian and cold.

And when No. 44 woke up, he knew what he had to do.

71

He saw Jordan Everstein in the yard and asked if he could have a word. Jordan looked to another guard for approval and was given a nod. He took No. 44 over to a corner near the fence, still in view of the guards on high and their automatic rifles. "What do you want?"

No. 44 told Jordan that he'd had a dream, and in this dream, he'd seen Jordan's house. He described it in detail: the chain-link fence, the small garden out front, the unfurnished basement. And then he told Jordan to tear down the west wall of his basement—a great fortune awaited him there, stored away by the previous owner prior to his untimely death, riches hidden behind the drywall. Jordan listened intently, and No. 44 could tell that he'd piqued his interest, hit that perfect flavor and flow—and No. 44 figured that this was the ideal place to end the conversation, and he went back towards the walking loop to get his steps in for the day. He knew that the worm of the idea was burrowing inside poor Jordan's head, and whether he dug through his wall tonight or tomorrow or in a week's or in a month's time, eventually, he'd cave to the idea and succumb to the task.

During the daily count, he noticed Jordan eyeing him warily; he never came over to speak with him, but his eyes rose up and down, appraising the man, trying to unearth whether or not some foul trick was at play, or whether good fortune had graced him with a prophesizing prisoner, foretelling riches untold and fame unforeseen, to be unearthed in his very own home.

It took three days for the worm to get the better of him, and he kissed his young wife one night, and he told her he needed to open up part of the basement wall, replace some insulation or whatnot. She smiled at her loving husband and let him go about his way. He smashed through the wall using a sledgehammer (taking note of the instructions No. 44 had given him, "About four feet in from the north-facing wall."), and he slotted his hands inside; he felt around and was surprised to find a recess going back a few feet. He reached in as far as he could and got hold of something; he pulled it out. Plastic sheets taped around a hefty device. He unwrapped it and found himself holding small bricks of cash in one-hundred-dollar denominations. He laid it out and counted it and found that he was the inheritor of close to six hundred thousand dollars. He let out a small yelp and called his wife down, and he swept her up in his arms and kissed her with greedy and joyous passion.

No. 44 did not see Jordan for a few days. He kept up with his routine of walking and waiting and talking to himself. He'd become quite adept at conversing with his brain and articulating rather fruitful conversations in the tangle of neurons comprising his mental hardware. Who was he? He figured it didn't matter much; it seemed irrelevant; he was a man fashioned by happy circumstances and bad luck and altered states. Definitions required the full picture in order to frame the subject accurately, and a man's full design could never be deduced until the final endnote was rung, denoted by his death. For a whole lifetime of filth and fury and disgust could go by and be redeemed in the final ten seconds (according to some), a strong ending redefining the entirety of the whole. Such miracles were not beyond the validity of reason, nor beyond the scope of redemption in some circles and sects. Life was strange, and in order to define it, one would have to see the entirety of the arc, put on the prescription glasses of a god, and see the full picture in all its bravura. And here he was, maybe two-thirds of the way through his second act (one could never really be sure), and he had no idea how to behave in accordance with how he would later be perceived (if he were ever thought of at all). The summary of his life would not concern him, and while he was here, he would play as many roles as he liked, venturing across the moral stratosphere of evil psychopaths and benign beggars; his life was his to shape and theirs to define. It was just the way it was.

72

"I don't trust no peoples," said Jordan Everstein's wife. "But I do trust some persons." Her name was Claire, and she was a lively brunette with a penchant for sundresses, her style highlighting the elegance of her petite female frame. Her jubilation at finding the cash had given way to panic. What now? Would someone come looking for it? Were they in trouble? What would the bank say? Jordan told her to calm down, stay sane, and keep focused on the gift (and all the positivity) they'd just received. God was looking out for them. And now she could quit her job at the dry cleaner's, and they could easily afford a child or two and an all-expenses-paid future (or, at the very least, a decade of frivolous ex-penditures). This made her smile ("Oh, darling..." she said); they walked upstairs and opened a bottle of white wine and made love and went to bed.

Claire dreamt that she'd gone down to the basement in the middle of the night and found Jordan standing over the money—the scene lit only by ambient moonlight entering in from the basement windows. He was making long, drawn-out moans, and when she got close, putting her hand on his shoulder, lovingly checking on her husband, he turned to reveal a face, carved up and leaking not only blood but some black malevolent substance too. She screamed, and he moaned, and then he raised his hand, and she saw he was holding a knife, and he cut a flap from his cheek, a loose piece of dangling flesh, and he ate it. She screamed—and his moans rose in pitch, and he tried to match her volume. She looked at the money stacked neatly at his feet, and then she woke up.

In the morning, she told him about her dream and his actions of self-mutilation and cannibalism, and then she cried; he tried to calm her, but she was inconsolable. She begged him to put the money back where he'd found it. It was cursed, she said. Jordan laughed and tried to reason with his wife, but she wouldn't stop crying. He went to work, and he didn't say a word to anyone about what he'd found, and when he saw No. 44, he avoided him and decided to never speak to him about the money, in fact, to pretend as if he (the prisoner) didn't exist—or to look at him as if he were just another regular asshole convict that he had to deal with, not the one who'd bestowed benediction and riches upon him and his wife. *Poor Claire*, he thought, his weak-willed wife melting away in a fit of imaginary guilt; she wasn't used to being gifted by the gods or fortune or prognosticating prisoners. She would come around, though. Surely, she would.

Jordan had a funny dream the next night. He dreamt he'd gone to his local corner store and bought a pack of cigarettes. He was discussing Roy Bradshaw's disastrous pitching with the clerk. He left, and in the parking lot, below the lamplight and the night sky, a hooded figure pressed up against him and poked a pistol into his side. "Give me your money, now," he said, and Jordan did as he was asked, and as he retrieved his wallet, he glanced into his car and saw the bundles of cash from the basement sitting in plain sight on his back seat. *Fuck*, he thought. He tried to distract the gunman and asked him what his intentions were holding up people in parking lots late at night. Surely there were easier and less risky ways to earn a living. The gunman laughed, and he said that it wasn't about the money—and as he talked, Jordan noticed a group of flies circling the man's head, like a halo of vermin, and Jordan waited as the man elucidated his point. "I am waging war... a war against heroes... against heroism," he said.

The gunman laughed again and paused and then said, "Well, aren't you gonna show me your haul in that there back seat?" Jordan sighed, and the gunman motioned to the car, and Jordan opened up the back door, and the gunman sprayed the cash with fluid and tossed in a match, and the back seat erupted in flames. They watched as the fire ate away at the interior of the car (scorched monetary ash drifted by the arsonist's ear); it poured out through the open door. And then the gunman raised the gun to his head and said, "It takes a surprising amount of courage to kill yourself. Don't you agree?"

"Just because you're shot or gay or have cancer or are a certain color or have so-and-so's number or have no head and no country or no brain or breast or breath doesn't allow you to be an asshole," said the clerk in the dream, while all Jordan ever wanted was his money back and a pack of smokes.

When he got back to the parking lot, he bent down and took the gunman's head (which had inexplicably come apart from his body), and now that he had no car, he decided to walk, and as he walked, he saw a refrigerator on the side of the road, and he opened the door and placed the head inside on the rack. He closed the fridge and sat down on the curb and thought about what it all might mean; a young girl walked up to him and said, "In order to fool anyone, you have to be able to fool yourself first. Channel the actor. Delude the wacko."

She opened the fridge and took the head.

He woke up in cold sweats.

At work the next day, Jordan was talking with another guard, and the guard told him that he was getting lots of *strange* lately. When Jordan asked what he meant, the guard looked at him as if he were an idiot and said, "Pussy, man. It means pussy."

73

A man knocked on the Eversteins' door Tuesday afternoon (3:14 p.m.) while Jordan was still at work; Claire was home, cooking and preparing food for the next few days. She answered the door in her apron, and the man, sporting a long trench coat and shiny black shoes, asked if he could speak with her for a moment. She asked what it was about, and he flashed his credentials (an inspector for the city), here to check on the sewage lines. "Could I come in and have a look?" She led him downstairs, and she told him about their renovations and to excuse the mess. The wall had yet to be patched up. The inspector poked around and went into the furnace room and checked on the ejector pump. It only took a minute, and he said everything looked fine. Claire thanked him and turned to go back upstairs (she was mulling over whether or not to offer him a cup of coffee), and then she heard a cough, and the inspector tumbled into a fit, and she asked if he was okay. He couldn't speak, and he fell to his knees and onto his side—his right hand rotated, and its interossei muscles collapsed and stiffened. She knelt beside him and patted his back; black fluid started to fall from his mouth. He got out the word *"water,"* and Claire ran upstairs to fetch some. When she returned, he was nowhere to be found, but in the corner of the room was a large bug. It was the size of a lobster—but it had the shape of a cockroach or a trilobite. She screamed and watched it turn; it crawled into the furnace room. She ran upstairs and slammed the basement door and called Jordan.

74

"There's nothing there."

He'd checked the furnace room and looked around the basement and found no evidence of man or bug. She swore she'd seen both, and when she went to bed, she took sleeping pills and swallowed a large glass of wine. Jordan was nervous for his wife. He kissed her on the forehead, damp with sweat, and he walked over to their closet and looked at the cash, safe and sound. He brushed his teeth and lay in bed. An hour later, he heard a bang coming from somewhere downstairs. He jolted awake and tried to raise Claire from her dreams, but she was sound asleep—dreaming of off-kilter killers and cream-colored sheep. He got up and walked downstairs, creeping slowly in the dark, trying to understand where the sound had come from. He checked their main floor, and everything seemed fine. He opened the basement door and edged down the stairs. They creaked under his weight, and he flipped on the light, and it all looked normal—except, he noted, for a small pile in the corner. He walked over to it, and it looked like vomit but full of other components and strings and linings and tendons. It smelt rank and raw, and he turned and noticed that the furnace room's door was open. He walked towards it, and he heard something scurry inside.

75

When the firefighters arrived at the scene, the house was beyond saving. Everyone inside had burned up; only the chain-link fence stood erect among the ruins.

76

"God was their director of photography."

No. 44 was visited by his old deviled self again—a blast of light and then the winged beast arrived in his cell, opening a heavenly portal on the wall; he flew in, and No. 44 glimpsed the trumpets and the heavens in the background along with fluffy, buoyant, pillowy clouds. "It's been done," said the devil. "Jordan Everstein is dead." No. 44 had no idea how this had happened; he'd pushed the first domino (planting the seed) but knew nothing beyond that, and the devil told him what had occurred; describing the tale, he left out no small detail, and although the story dragged on somewhat, No. 44 was happy to have a fine storyteller like his old deviled self to spin a good yarn while he sat immobilized in captivity. He'd longed for an entertaining chronicle, a slice of good ol' Americana, and the devil had delivered, and the plan had worked. Number 59 was crossed off the list—but No. 44 still had questions, and he asked the devil about his strategy

("Why so many hoops, man?"). How come they couldn't just keep it simple (poison the jailer's coffee)? Why were they dabbling in all this malarkey? These excessive shenanigans? And the devil responded, saying that in order to orchestrate anything in this life, it required delicacy, like ornate origami, folded thousands of times with care and precision, each fold calculated, each cause and effect mapped out, because sometimes there is only one way to precipitate the events forward to that desired final shape; and it may be long and hard and arduous and nonsensical, and it will almost certainly be made up of seemingly indirect movements working towards that common end—in this case, the death of Jordan Everstein (a temporary shape, a soon-to-be-renewed shape... a shape drifting outward... drifting somewhere... folding, pleating, puckering, expanding... but *where*?).

"And I'm a sucker for unruly plots with sharp turns and strange zigzagging formations. Art lies in the roundabout trip, full of misdirection and misgivings, not necessarily in the most efficient and direct route," spoke the devil. And No. 44 wasn't entirely sure if he agreed, but he partially did.

77

"Sometimes, it's the devil inside that shows us the way out."

He hated goodbyes; he found them ridiculous. He had long ago bid the world farewell. Only the husk of a farce remained. It was still sad though, but it was also a bit funny and fatuous and off-putting. The devil told him that it was time (a prison break!), and that night, much like in the vision he'd had, the devil opened up a portal in his cell, but this time, No. 44 stepped through it, following the devil, and he appeared in a grassy field filled with metallic debris at an aging train station somewhere in a southern county. The sun was going down, and tears crowded his eyes as he took in the beauty of the wide-open space. The devil stood beside him, and the two of them sat on a rusty oil drum, and the devil offered No. 44 a cigar, and No. 44 accepted and smoked and blew rings as echoes of the surrounding world made their way to their eardrums; they were quiet, smiling and smoking. "Get some rest," said the devil. "Tomorrow's another beautiful day."

78

Number 60 was George Leloup, an obese man who lived in the woods alone, his shirt stained with grease and his breath colored by the unmistakable stench of rot; No. 44 and the devil had decided to walk there, it being only a stone's throw from the train station. They conversed and strolled, eyed some feral cats, and stopped at a small restaurant attached to a gas station called Mira's Meals to eat.

When they got to George's place, it was late afternoon, and they knocked on the door, and George opened up—and the friendly fellow invited them in. He led them through the shack and out towards an area with a makeshift BBQ and an old picnic table. No. 44 watched as a spider moved nimbly across its web, already having conquered the terrain with numerous bugs and meals and half-devoured corpses scattered across its trap. No. 44 studied George; he seemed like a decent fellow—and although No. 44 felt little remorse killing a middle-aged, backwoods hillbilly, he felt it necessary to do so quickly and in as merciful a manner as possible. He let George ramble on about God and his shrine and his prayer log out back, and as he turned and walked into the woods to relieve himself, No. 44 snuck up and, using a banana knife he'd nicked from a nearby shed, sliced his throat and bled him and let him tumble through the thicket and roll down to the bottom of the brook.

"All done?" asked the devil.

No. 44 nodded, and the devil told him that he wanted to show him something, and he opened another portal, and the two of them stepped through.

79

They arrived in hell, and they stood on a ledge overlooking a giant crater overrun by people fighting in what seemed to be a savage battle, and the devil said that these were the everyday, normal sinners; regular bozos and boring nobodies that hell had swallowed up and forced to combat one another over trivial nonsense for eternity: a hell of their own design. And the devil said, "Watch this," and he clapped his hands and gazed upwards and mumbled some jibber-jabber and clapped again, and all of a sudden, the armies all stopped—as if manipulated by some invisible puppeteer—and each combatant swung in unison, synchronized deathblows littered the battleground (wielding axe, sword, or mace), Pyrrhic victories everywhere, resulting in hack-and-slash lunacy across the board, and thus canceling everyone out of the game. For those few who hadn't been struck by a decisive blow, the remainders each unsheathed a knife from their belts and cut out their own tracheas. The entire battlefield lay dead, and No. 44 thought back to his youth, when he used to play Tetris on the toilet—and about how he'd line everything up and sometimes get that perfect shape at the perfect time and destroy the entirety of the screen. The log floating perfectly down, or a fresh start, or a fucking nuke bomb redefining the scope of the game.

"That's a nifty trick," said No. 44.

"'Tis," said the devil.

80

They were a buddy comedy—the devil and No. 44—strolling the land and jumping through portals and offing targets and laughing and eating and hanging out and living their best lives. The devil clapped No. 44 on the back and grinned at his cohort. They had just killed Amanda Goodwin, and No. 44 was cleaning off some of her brains that had snuck their way into his beard. He reloaded the shotgun and slung it over his shoulder, and he looked at the devil and realized he loved his friend. *Friends until the end*, thought No. 44, and he asked his pal if they could take a little vacation. Halt the killing for a little bit; enjoy the relaxing scenery of the Spanish coast or the Patagonian wilderness. The devil thought this sounded like a fine idea. They'd worked hard and were already at number 66, arriving in a relatively short span of time—their skills now exceeding the requirements of the task. A vacation sounded like a splendid plan, and the devil opened up a portal, and No. 44 hopped in.

81

They arrived at the Rio Sands, a hotel backing onto a sprawling beach—men in Hawaiian shirts hawking paddleboats and kayaks, grinning tourists, food stands selling burgers and cotton candy (and sometimes calamari...), and menus scribbled across sunbaked chalkboards. It was all umbrellas and brats and beautiful women and angry young fathers. They were on the balcony of a twelfth-floor suite. No. 44 looked around the room and admired the craftsmanship and the wood finishing and the two bedrooms with en-suite facilities.

He returned to the balcony and found the devil, still there, gazing at the richness of the azure world. Tourists and locals busied themselves on the sand and in the lapping waves; the screams of laughter and playfulness developed and formed a cohesive chorus. No. 44 felt safe and relaxed, and he sat sipping orange juice and scarfing down bacon and eggs, all of which had miraculously appeared on a fabulous metallic cart. "What do you think?" asked the devil—his horns dripped sweat, and the air was thick, and humidity prevailed; No. 44 signaled his approval. It was just what he'd wanted.

82

"A god wants but never needs (and often has to wait a really fucking long while, anyway)."

They headed down to the restaurant to grab some more food and check out the lay of the land and were met by an astute waiter with prominent front teeth. They ordered the catch of the day and ate and gawked; and the other guests entered and exited—beach supplies in tow.

A filthy man stood on the other side of the road; he was taping messages to pigeons' feet, and No. 44 watched with great interest as he sent yet another winged message out into the world.

They didn't do much besides sit by the water and eat and converse for the next few days. They were friendly with the staff and the other beachgoers, and the devil incorporated himself into a group of young people, and one night, they all went out to a club, and one of the girls, Daphne, edged up to No. 44 on the dance floor, and before he knew it, they were kissing and making out, hands pulling and clutching one another. They left before the others and went swimming. She looked up at one point and said something in Italian and smiled, and No. 44 noticed she was missing a tooth. The Big Dipper was clearly visible above her head, and she asked him what he did for a living, and he said that he and the devil were in the insurance game. He wasn't sure why he'd said that, and he laughed, and afterwards, he kissed her again.

He walked her back to her hotel and continued alone along the beach; he scratched at his thinning hair and hummed "Ave Maria," and he saw the man who'd been taping messages to pigeons' feet spread-eagle, sprawled near the water; he wondered if he was okay or dead or asleep. He shuffled back towards his room and took the elevator up, and he saw the devil partaking in a gravity-defying threesome with two girls from the club. The TV was on, showing an American sitcom dubbed in Spanish (volume blaring, "*Sólo un poco por favor!*"): it was a super-natural fuck-fest full of magic and moans and vibrators and laugh tracks.

When he got up, the two girls were still there, asleep on displaced couches, breasts exposed, a sea of ruffled linen, feathers floating and bougie debris scattered about. The devil said good morning, and No. 44 tipped his hat and went down to the hotel's restaurant to eat. He picked up a book at a little shop and rounded the bend and spent the morning out on the sand reading and watching the kids and families overtake the beach. "Get back here! *Goddamnit!*" yelled some father at his six-year-old son. The devil came by a little while later, smiling and asking No. 44 how his vacation was going. They both agreed that the rest and the reprieve were doing them well, but after a few more days, they'd return to

the kill list and knock off the final thirty-three-odd murders
that awaited them.

83

As the day wore on, No. 44 found himself aimless and already itching to get back to the hunt. He'd grown accustomed to it, and even though he was prone to taking breaks and sabbaticals, he found himself, more than ever, hungry for an assignment. He enjoyed the relaxing and meandering life of a tourist or beachgoer or degenerate, but inevitably, after a couple of days, he'd grow bored and low-grade anxiety would creep in, asking him, sometimes gently and sometimes not, what he was doing, wasting away, pretending he was one of them—an ordinary Joe or a regular John—when, in fact, he was anything but.

He caught his partner in the room snacking on some room service, and the devil explained that the next kill (number 66) was a real doozy. "Make sure you rest up," said the devil. "It'll take all your cunning and malevolence to off that sombitch."

So, they spent their last few days like those that had come before, lounging at the beach and eating at restaurants and watching TV, and No. 44 thought back to the prison and the repetition and drew parallels with the resort. He went for a walk, and when he got back to his room, he saw the devil eating again, and when he looked closer, he saw he was nibbling on someone's foot, severed below the ankle, blood dripping from his mouth, and the devil said that he'd miss this place, and then he took another bite and washed it down with a few gulps of beer.

84

According to the list, Baal was next. They'd checked out of the hotel and said their goodbyes, and outside, they walked along the beach one last time until they got to a sparse section near an estuary, and the devil cast his spell, and the portal appeared, and he motioned to No. 44 as if to say, "After you." And No. 44 hopped through the portal, and it was dark, and he noticed he was in a large cave, presumably underground, with great walls and ceilings and giant spires and stalactites hanging overhead. A massive lake reached out, and water covered most of the ground (a cavernous oasis), and he and the devil stood on an outlying perimeter of stone, and No. 44 crouched on the bank and dipped his hands into the lake, and the devil watched him do it.

They heard a sound and then a rumbling, and the water started to bubble, and way off, near the middle of the lake, a giant three-headed figure appeared, unearthed itself and drew breath. It had the head of a man and a cat and a toad, and all three heads made sounds in unison before the head of the man spoke.

"Why do you disturb me, you tiny, meager fuck?"

No. 44 was surprised and visually taken aback; he'd had no idea that anything akin to whatever-the-hell-Baal-was could be included on this *godforsaken* list. He thought back to Wayne, the shark, but this was something else entirely—something mythical and strange and demonic. How the hell was he supposed to kill Baal, anyway, the three-headed *fucking* brute?

"Hello," said No. 44; and as he tried to think of something to say, he searched his person for any kind of weapon and realized he hadn't brought anything with him. He looked at the devil, hoping that he had a knife or a gun or a bazooka on hand. The devil, knowing exactly what No. 44's look insinuated, tossed him a .38, and without thinking, No. 44 aimed at Baal and pulled the trigger in rapid succession. Bam. Bam. Bam. And Baal laughed.

"Silly bastard," said Baal. "You think you can defeat me like that?" And he rose up, out of the water, uncovering himself and exposing a slimy torso, rotting and putrid and huge. No. 44 looked at the devil for advice, but he just shrugged. Baal came closer, parting the waters and making great waves, and No. 44 stood still, uncertain what to do.

When he came around, he was tied to a chair. Little bald minions stood around him, jutting out painted chins—clad in tattered undies—and making cackling and hissing sounds. Baal sat before him: an immense figure, fifty or sixty feet tall, he sat cross-legged, all three heads staring at him.

"Wakey-wakey, little friend."

A red glow colored the pale rock of the scene, and No. 44 looked down at his battered and bloodstained body, gashed and ripped apart.

No. 44 turned his head and tried to see the devil, but he couldn't find any sign of him, and when he looked up, he saw Baal in the midst of monologizing. Twisting and turning, dancing from one strange sentence to the next.

And then he was off—out he went, dozing away ("oh, heavenly unconscious"), and No. 44 fell back asleep, due to the pain, the tiredness, or Baal's weary voice? And then... heat, pressure, pain and he jolted awake; the minions were cutting into him, sharp rocks redefining his look, and he yelled, and Baal laughed, and No. 44 wondered about the devil... and about how he was going to get out of this mess.

During his torture (which ran the gamut from major to minor), No. 44 realized that he wasn't necessarily good or bad—just an animal with lots of illusions, playing the part of youthful savage in a savage and tedious game. And during the entirety of his torture, Baal read out his sins, starting with his more wrathful and violent and murderous ones, and then fanning out to the lesser (although still sinful) deeds scattered throughout his checkered past (theft and betrayal and sodomy and such—with Baal even including the masturbatory transgressions of his teenage years). He couldn't tell whether the pain of Baal's jejune voice or the agonizing wounds inflicted a more dismal fate.

It was during a semi-lucid moment that No. 44 heard Baal discuss amongst its varied heads whether or not they should eat him. The cat was all for it, but the toad opposed the idea, and the man couldn't make up his mind. They argued awhile, and No. 44 drifted in and out of consciousness before being roused once more, in the clutches of Baal, and then he was tossed up and into the air and caught in the mouth of the cat and sliding down its esophagus and into the vat of its gut.

85

It was fucked up in there. He looked around, and his eyes had trouble adjusting. Gastric juice sat at the base of the stomach, and No. 44 crouched on some random protrusion of organ and thought about what to do. He saw the remains of some entity smoldering in its final fit before being washed down and carried over into the small intestine. He was hungry and looked around for anything resembling food, and he searched his pockets and found a pack of matches he'd snagged while at the resort. He pulled some hair from the crumpled-up corpse and tried to concoct a small fire atop his area. He blew softly into the flames, and they rose, and the smell of charred hair perfumed his confined quarters. He pulled at a loose bit from the lining of the wall; it came away, and he roasted it on the fire. He ate well, and as he was finishing up, he felt Baal cough—and the whole of the stomach bounced up and down and him along with it. He witnessed the corpse on the floor bend in half, and then it was sucked further along. He was the preeminent voyeur of Baal's digestive tract.

86

He only had a couple of matches left, and it was getting hard to breathe, and the smell inside of Baal was atrocious. In a moment of abject misery, No. 44 stripped off his clothes and prepared himself to lie on the floor near the orifice that would further him along in his journey and end his fate once and for all. And then, like a lightning strike or meteor slamming into Earth, No. 44 had an idea. He piled his clothes in a corner of the hollow organ and lit a match: they caught fire fast, and the smoke started to rise, and No. 44 tore at anything loose he could find to add to the growing bonfire; horrible rumbles started, and amid the sound, the trampoline of Baal's stomach moved up and down, coughing fits erupted, and the fire spread; as No. 44 was being burned alive in the pit of Baal, he laughed, and everything went black as water was poured in from Baal's many mouths and smoke rose up—and then he saw an opening and the glint of a blade. Baal, in the madness of pain, had cut into its stomach, and No. 44 pushed and prodded and pulled at the flap of severed flesh; and, through

a form of botched cesarean, he emerged, covered in goo, burnt
and naked and exhausted. And there the devil was, standing
before him, staring at him, with words of encouragement no
less. "A fine job, son. A fine job indeed."

87

Why the hell were they still doing this? What was the point of this continuous struggle? This bitter sweepstakes and these unnecessary kills? And the devil looked at him and said that sometimes you should simply greet the world with a scream, awaken your dark desires and release them in rapturous wails. A man facing down these odds need not contend himself with rational modes of thought: it could no longer supply the answers; doom was looming, and the realms of the ecstatic and the mad were the best places to squat for the time being. And then there was always the hope of peace, and No. 44 asked the devil where he could find this peace, and the devil told him that he could find it in death. Death was peace, but most people didn't want that or didn't see it that way. They were mired by the need to wage war and exist in conflict, even in trivial and small ways, for an eternity if they could. "If death is peace, then man has no greater enemy than its sickening silence and ugly stillness," said the devil.

88

"He couldn't control time, so he grappled with space and tried to possess as much as possible."

They hopped through the portal again and found themselves in a rustic, desert milieu. They walked beneath the sweltering sun and saw an encampment or hamlet or small town through the haze a couple of miles off. As they neared, No. 44 was reminded of the great western films of his youth, a pompous sheriff and a posse of scoundrels and no-good vagrant types, defining the terms of justice with lead bullets and a slack or sickening gaze. He felt rumblings in his gut and had to scurry behind a bush to evacuate his bowels while the devil walked on, slowing his pace.

The devil spotted a coyote walking across the land, its head turned in his direction, and he offered a salutation of sorts, but he only succeeded in scaring the creature off. He looked up at the sky and had to squint and touched his horns; they were warm and bore small cracks. He sat on the hard caliche and waited for his friend to reappear. He looked back at him and saw him tightening his belt and refastening his buckle. He was all cut up and wild and ragged, and the devil listened to the cicadas and closed his eyes.

"So, where are we?"

"A place called Dutton," said the devil.

"Is number 67 here?"

"I think so."

They walked over to the hotel, and they each got a room. The saloon stood across the road, and they wandered over for a drink and were greeted by card-playing miners and dolled-up whores. A barmaid brought them a bottle of unmarked whiskey, and the fellow next to them spit tobacco on the floor. The devil handed No. 44 the .38 underneath the table, and he was once again happy to be in possession of a firearm. *Under such conditions, a man without a gun ain't no man at all,* thought No. 44. They looked at the list and spotted number 67; she was listed as Isabella Blue. The devil said she was one of the whores upstairs. The easiest way would be to pay for her company and then escape out the window afterwards. He (the devil) would stay down here and nurse the whiskey and keep an eye out for any trouble. No. 44 went up to the barkeep and asked about Isabella, and the barkeep waved over the madam, and No. 44 paid her, and she led him upstairs towards a room where a girl sat waiting on the edge of a bed. She was young, and when she looked at him, a pang of sadness shot through him. She was beautiful and broken, and No. 44 wished it wasn't her name that appeared on the list. The madam left, and Isabella got undressed; she didn't say a word; she looked shy and dispirited. No. 44 didn't speak; he felt horrible. He asked her where she was from, and she said, "Here." He asked her if she'd turn around and face the wall while he undressed; she did as she was asked. She turned slowly, and he leveled the gun, and he hesitated a moment, and then he fired. He jumped through the window, and he and the devil had to fight their way out of town, and he was wounded by the spray of a shotgun, and the devil was shot in its claw. And then the devil extended its wings and rose up and carried the man who'd shot him into the air and gripped his head and pulled it off, and then he threw it at the crowd. This seemed to scare them off, and they dispersed, and the two beasts were able to get back to the hotel and grab their things unmolested by the mob. No. 44 didn't speak, and neither did the devil, and they wandered off into the desert.

Their wounds forced them to rest a couple of miles out. And they made a small fire while No. 44 dug the pellets out from his ribs, and the devil wrapped his injured hand. In the middle of the night, No. 44 woke up and saw two glowing bulbs and growling fangs; he stared into them until the wolf grew bored and continued on its way.

He had trouble getting back to sleep, and the devil snored and breathed deeply.

89

"God favors little children, drunks, and shortsighted gamblers."

"I question the sincerity of all things," said the devil. "Man's will is a tangle of insanities rooted in unknown causes, with a single blind force pushing it towards unknown ends. How can anyone trust something as deceptive as the human mind?"

No. 44 shrugged and didn't reply. He threw small stones at the carcass of last night's fire; he'd barely slept, and his head felt heavy and dull. They didn't do much that day, and they sat beneath the sun, and the devil kept his eye out for the coyote, and in the afternoon, he saw him, and he flew over to him. When he landed, the coyote froze, and the devil tried to offer it some food. He tried to appear small and meek, but the coyote ran off in the opposite direction, and the devil raised his gun and fired into the air and yelled, "Get!" He went back to No. 44, who looked morose and lost, and the devil could see that the list and the kills were getting to him. Instead of becoming easier, the task had somehow become harder. Initially, in the beginning, the task seemed undemanding, easy enough, and for a time, even grew easier, and then, after a while, it went in the opposite direction and grew harder and was now a great burden. The devil wondered how he could help his friend—relieve some of the pain and pressure, but he couldn't come up with any plausible solutions. He lay and slept and dreamt, and he dreamt of a woman who asked him to remove his clothes, and he did this, and he did it eagerly and happily, and then she asked him to remove more, and she handed him a knife, and the devil cut off bits of his flesh, and the woman wanted more, and the devil cut out bigger chunks (he even sawed off his horns)... and still, she wanted more. The devil took out his organs and cut off his appendages, and he was left gutted (no more than the torso of a sickly, malformed skeleton), and the woman said *more*, and then the devil woke up, and he shuddered beneath the blistering sun, and he watched as the ants dragged the corpse of a centipede across the crust of the land bound together with clay and silt.

90

The fog was thick, and the streetlights threw off a diffused glow, and No. 44 had no idea if it was night or day or some hellish in-between time.

Where had the portal taken them?

He had trouble seeing more than ten feet in front of him, and he and the devil kept close to one another. They heard the electrical buzz from a large neon sign and entered through the door beneath it. The convenience store clerk stared at them but didn't say anything. The devil went over and bought himself a slushy and a pack of cigarettes.

"Heavy fog out there. When's it supposed to lift, mister?"

The clerk shrugged and gave the devil back his change, and then he stared up at a TV showing a looped ten-second segment; a man laughed at another man for reasons unknown. They got out of there, and the devil said, "This place gives me the creeps," and No. 44 had to agree. They walked through the gloom and the murk and through a park (accented by dark spruces) and heard the sound of some kid singing some rhyme; they heard the rhythmic beats of a skipping rope, but no person or rope ever appeared. They kept on and saw another glowing sign and entered below it and climbed the stairs and entered a reception area, and No. 44 spoke to the woman behind the desk, and he got them two rooms and a bellhop in maroon dress escorted them up the hotel's winding staircase. And No. 44 turned on the TV; it showed the same looped scene from the convenience store. He sat on the bed and watched it and acquiesced to its pace.

91

When they exited the hotel in the morning, the weather remained largely unchanged. They walked over to a coffee shop and got two coffees to go, and No. 44 and the devil walked towards an empty parking lot and entered through automatic doors and found themselves in the town's mall. The gloom did not dissipate inside but seemed to have taken on a new consistency. Fluorescent lights and a hazy cast of pinks and greens assaulted them through the corridors as dazed shoppers shuffled from one outlet to the next. Near the center of the mall was a skating rink, and the two fellas watched as a young girl practiced her choreographed routine to atonal soundscapes.

"So, who's next?" asked No. 44.

"Jonathan Dumont. He works at the school. I figure we head over there in the early evening and get it over with and get the hell out of here."

No. 44 agreed, and they walked through the mall and bought some snacks, and the devil got himself a brand-new pair of shorts.

They went back to the hotel in the afternoon, and No. 44 was drowsy and kept looking out the window at the fog, thinking he saw tentacles in the distance, and he heard a constant commotion of electrical interference from some unknown source. *What kind of town was this?* thought No. 44. A strange fucking place, to be sure. He flicked on the TV and sat back and went through the channels until he came across one that looked like a security feed—and then he saw the devil, in grainy black and white, in his hotel room, sitting on the bathroom floor, and a strange liquid-like ooze was creeping towards him. The devil was unaware, and No. 44 shouted at the TV ("Turn around!"), and the ooze shot out and gripped him and spread all over him. He seized up and struggled, and No. 44 ran (arriving in a jiff), and he knocked on his friend's door, and the devil answered, and he looked none the worse for wear, and No. 44 asked if he was all right, and the devil said that he was, and then the devil asked him what he thought of his new shorts, and he did a little spin that made them both smile.

92

They went to the pool hall around 2 p.m., and No. 44 had forgotten how much he enjoyed the game, and he and the devil played for a while before being interrupted by some rude fat-fella types, and No. 44 played against the loudest of the bunch and won two hundred dollars off him; the fat man wanted to play again, and the devil told him to fuck off. They finished their beers and ventured towards the school around 4 p.m., and the devil examined his hand—his wound from their Wild West showdown had gotten worse; it looked infected, and No. 44 thought about his injured ribs... and about how little they'd been bothering him of late. He shivered for some reason, and the fog loomed thick. They stepped onto the school's pitch and saw some straggling kids immersed in thoughts of someone's design, staring up at the mist.

The receptionist told them that they'd just missed Jonathan. "Rats!" said the devil, and they walked through the empty hallways lined with lockers and dim orange-brown lighting.

They made their way through the gymnasium and out a side door, and the devil checked the list again and got the address from the database. The fog was too thick for them to fly, and the devil recommended that they get a taxi. They found a yellow cab sitting across the street, and the two mercenaries hailed it and squeezed in.

"Howdy, strangers. Where can I take you boys?"

He drove them outside the city center, and No. 44 watched out the window as plants like he'd never seen emerged in glimpses out of the thicket. The mist had turned a sickly blue, and the trees bore no leaves and instead were perched and populated with shapeless fruits bursting and hanging, cocooned sacs of red fluid with thick blue veins running throughout. An animal with antlers rushed by; it seemed both diseased and horny.

They turned around a bend, and the cab stopped at a long gravel driveway and let them out. No. 44 paid the driver, and he slammed the gas and spit rocks their way.

They walked towards the house; a barn or garage stood on the left, and the driveway forked. They rang the doorbell, and a man with prominent facial deformities answered. The distortions seemed to have enlarged his head and blurred his features, as if the cast of his face had melted long before it had had time to set. The lid of one eye hung entirely over the eyeball, and his mouth drooped, and he asked them what they wanted.

"To have a word," said the devil, and Jonathan made room for them to come inside.

They sat at the dining room table, and Jonathan brought them each a beer, and No. 44 looked out the window and saw an elk feasting on the bulbous ganglions of the cocooned fruit.

"So, what can I do for you, gentlemen?" asked Jonathan.

They made up a fib and asked him about his property, and if he ever thought about offering it up for sale. He smiled, and because of his facial eccentricities, it was hard for the devil and No. 44 to guess what he was thinking. Then he pounded his fists on the table, and he seemed to get angry.

"Do you know how many *assholes* come here every year? Try to burn me? Buy this place? Offer up small fortunes? Eat up my time?"

The devil was not feeling the man's rant, and his beer was almost finished, and he signaled to No. 44 to hurry up and get it over with. No. 44 grabbed his beer bottle and smacked Jonathan over the head, and Jonathan went down, and then No. 44 pulled out his .38 Special and finished the job. The hole in Jonathan's head distorted his features further, and No. 44 knew that he'd never, in all his life, get rid of that image—the small man with a strange skull, split open and spewing.

They sat on Jonathan's deck afterwards and grabbed another beer and watched the sunset and the great testicular globs of vegetation sway among the branches; No. 44 could swear he saw blurs of movement among the woods, like mosquitoes but a meter high, traveling at breakneck speed. The devil opened up the portal, and they hopped in.

93

They arrived at some unknown city's downtown and glimpsed skyscrapers and rush hour and beautiful women in evening dresses. They stopped at a posh tavern and ordered a bottle of wine, and No. 44 ordered the beef bourguignon, and the devil ordered *coq au vin*. They sat quietly and ate and drank and admired the shift in tone, the normalcy—or normalcy personified by what the twenty-first century defined it as. Another diner knocked over his glass of wine, and a sudden crash arrested the scene, and then No. 44 saw the saucier flip a passing guest the bird. There was an intricate game of chaos being played out in the vestibule and main arteries of this establishment, and No. 44 had no way of orienting himself within it. Events floated by unconnected to one another; he drifted through the world unable to grasp its overarching concepts or schemes. It was going too fast, and the people were nothing but a blur, a sideshow to his mission. He wondered if this was what was meant by dehumanization, and then an old man brushed up against him, and he felt like kicking his head in.

They stole a car outside the restaurant from an inattentive valet. The devil got in (folding his wings just so) and drove. They hightailed it down a narrow alleyway and skidded onto the main drag. According to the devil, their 69th victim, Brian Rampart, was dining right now, so they had some time to kill. They parked near the pier, and the devil got out and lit a smoke, and No. 44 followed suit, and they sat on the hood, and No. 44 could smell the distinct odor of the sea: pungent and salty.

"Nice night," said the devil, and No. 44 agreed.

"All right, time to shine," said the devil. "You drive."

They drove through the main channels of the city and took a left on Dufreud Drive, and the devil pointed to a well-dressed man in a sharp suit. He was getting into a car with a tall woman, and the devil said, "That's him," and No. 44 slowed down and edged over to the curb, and once they started off, he followed behind. The devil flicked on the radio, and the voice said, "*Up next on KJLA, a classic from Milli Vanilli... after a word from our sponsors...*"

The roads were wet, and the mirroring posed a problem for No. 44; the traffic lights and high-rise lights reflected off the glossy ground and were hypnotic and impeded his focus. He felt it all blurring together, and then the walls closed in, and he heard the devil yelling at him; his mind unplugged from his circuit board, and then his vision went black (blurred, ebony cathedrals... and the fading city towers), and his body fell limp. Darkness washed over him, and it had no bottom.

When he came to, he was in the hospital. His head hurt like a motherfucker, and he could see the scrapes and bruises on his knees where his hospital gown ended. A nurse came by, and she asked how he was (her demeanor: sweet but reticent), and he said not bad, and he asked her what'd happened, and she said he'd been in a car accident, and he asked about his friend (the devil), and the nurse's face grew solemn, and she said he'd passed away. She grew awkward and fidgeted and then left.

No. 44's eyes exploded with tears.

94

He was released after four days and was considered lucky by the healthcare professionals for having survived such a crash. Apparently, they'd been hit by a drunken motorist speeding through an intersection; she'd slammed into the passenger side of the car, crushing the devil, folding him into the metallic frame and ejecting No. 44 out the window; he'd rolled and luckily evaded most obstructions. No. 44 asked if he could see the devil, and they took him down to the hospital's basement, to the morgue, and they pulled the devil out of the wall, and there wasn't much left of him on the tray beneath the covering, his face replete with wounds and contusions and his horns busted and broken off; his lower extremities were nowhere to be found, and his wings had been clipped. *Poor bastard*, thought No. 44, and he took the elevator and exited the hospital and got himself a hotel room close by, and he closed the curtains and slept and stayed in for five days. His room was on the eighth floor; it had a decent view.

95

He had the list back. They had given him the devil's belongings at the hospital, and he logged on to the database via his phone. Brian Rampart lived on Maplewood Drive, and No. 44 grabbed some tinfoil from an old takeout meal and taped it around his knuckles. He hailed a cab and gave the driver Brian's address.

He didn't care who was home. He was going to beat him to death with his bare paws, and although it was an irrational response, Brian would serve as his outlet. *Why?* Because No. 44 was alone... again, and therefore, Brian would bear the brunt of his frustration and share in his hurt; he would multiply it and transmute it, turn his pain into violence. He knocked, but no one answered.

He went around back and peeked in through a window and saw light. He lifted the window and crept inside. He walked through the house and eased doors open and checked the rooms—but he couldn't find anyone. He opened the basement door and went down the steps. And still no one.

He heard a sound and swung around and noticed light coming from the end of the hall, a door ajar. He moved towards it and looked through the gap. He saw a man holding a child and reading to it and rocking it and soothing it. He listened awhile and heard a story about a frog and a scorpion. When the story was done, he went back upstairs and stole a Pop-Tart from Brian's kitchen and left out a window. He walked around for most of the night and sat down on an anonymous patch of grass. He looked up at the stars, and when he got up, his pants were wet from the dew.

96

He was losing it, or so he thought. His killer instincts were waning. He rented a car and followed Brian around the next day. He sat outside Brian's work and watched him interact with his coworkers and clients and eat fettuccine Alfredo for lunch. He followed him afterwards and saw him enter a warehouse on the outskirts of the city; he kept his distance and followed him to a toy store downtown. He idled behind him at a traffic light, and his teeth finally came back to the fore, and he stomped hard on the gas and pushed Brian out into the intersection. Both his and Brian's vehicles were hit in the ensuing crash (a woman and her husband had T-boned Brian, and Brian's car had pushed back into his, and another vehicle had swerved and hit No. 44). When the dust finally settled, No. 44 got out. There was blood coming out from one of his eyes, and he could taste heavy metals in his mouth. He walked over to Brian's window; he was passed out or dead, and No. 44 pulled out his .38 and shot Brian in the head. He walked for a couple of blocks, and then he

stole some kid's bike and pedaled off down an unknown
street.

97

He got a plane ticket a few days later and went back to his home with the Overman and the garage and the mounted alligator head. He wanted a base of operations, or perhaps just a link to his past—however arbitrary it was. He figured that with the help of the Overman, he could stay put and get the list done in as quiet and tranquil a manner as he was likely to find.

He opened the door, and he lay on his couch and cried, and then he looked up and saw the alligator head and stared at it for a long time. He slept on the floor that night, and in the morning, he saw his neighbor Joe Dunlop, and he waved at him through the window, but Joe didn't see him; he scrutinized the glass pane.

He tried texting Wendy the next day but received no reply. He walked around and felt himself re-entering an older life; a slice from his past reinserted into his present, transplanted, as if all that had come between (the prison and the devil and the deaths) were all some fabricated dream, non-entities existing in non-space, and now he was back, living his authentic life. It felt good to recalibrate back here, and he sat on his sofa and watched TV and ate some mac and cheese.

He wondered if life was a zero-sum game.

That night he dreamt that he was a racecar driver, and he lost every race for ten years straight (not one *goddamn* stinking win!); and one race, he got all turned around and went ass-backwards and was forced to drive in reverse. He was surprised to find that he was far superior in reverse; he was an ass-backwards driver. He won. It was a good dream.

98

He walked out to the Overman in his boxers carrying a cup of coffee. The binder was lying where he'd left it, and he grabbed a snippet of number 70's hair and slotted it into the machine. The familiar rush greeted him and pulled him in. He felt excited.

Jennifer Buckwheat was seated outside in a field. There was a wooden table and four chairs; she sat there alone. The sun was going down, and the leaves were a vibrant yellow and red. He looked over the autumnal scene and saw a house in the distance. Jack-o'-lanterns stood on its porch; it was the magic hour, and No. 44 figured he'd sit with Jennifer for a minute. He wandered over and sat down.

"Hello."

"Hi."

"Whatcha doing out here?"

"I'm looking for my cat"—she pointed to the field without looking—"she's run off."

No. 44 looked at the field. *It would be hard to find a cat in there*, he thought, and the wheat shook to the pulse of the wind; and any small creature would surely remain hidden in the swaying stalks—concealed indefinitely.

"I'm sure she'll turn up," said No. 44, and Jennifer said nothing; she turned and looked at the field, her expression mute.

"Why are you here?" she asked.

"Just because, I guess."

"Hmm."

He sat with her awhile longer. They were quiet. He didn't feel like killing her. And then he left.

He went to the Overman and hung out with Jennifer three more times. He was lonely, and he liked her, and he didn't feel in any rush to end it. He looked forward to seeing her, and one time, they were in a boat, and she fell out, and she was drowning, and she looked to No. 44 for help, but he didn't move; he watched her, and the scene shook, and her body sank, and he imagined the exit, and he got the hell out of there.

99

No. 44 walked to the kitchen and got himself a plastic bag, and he dumped in some paint thinner and hobby glue; he added in a towel. He sat on the couch and put the bag to his mouth and huffed the fumes and took many deep breaths. *Death by 1,000 paper cuts*, he thought. He inhaled again and checked the movie channels and then laid his head back and stared up at nothing in particular.

He grabbed a pipe and smoked some drug that he couldn't recall the name of. The ceiling started to disappear, and fractal patterns maneuvered about; he saw God, or he felt Him, or he confused Him with a chemical aberration, and then he was moving at warp speed into some infinite tesseract. Squares were both expanding and shrinking, and the images were illuminating, and he felt like his brain was rolling backwards. He wondered if he was having a stroke, and then everything normalized, and the TV was showing a large woman waxing her shins. She kept smiling at the screen with her great big jowls.

100

He started killing fast and hard, and he rushed to complete as much as he could over the next couple of days. In a week, he killed number 71 through 77. He simply dropped into the Overman and butchered them. Frustrations aside, he felt pretty good—he was a machete-wielding madman losing the last shred of whatever constituted his humanity. He barked instead of talked; he shuffled instead of walked. He knew he'd gone too far, but alas, what was he to do? There was no road back, only a blank canvas—all directions open, all paths equally irrelevant. He spun around and danced and praised and cursed the skies. He was approaching madness at warp speed; it was an eerie feeling.

He took out his .38 one night and sat in the garage with the door closed. *God, was he tired.* He didn't even think about it. It just happened. He placed the gun to his head and pulled the trigger. It was that easy.

101

When he opened his eyes, he saw the devil. He wasn't surprised that the end wasn't the end. Evil seemed to be embedded in the continuous strife he was unable to extricate himself from.

"Hi, No. 44."

"Hi, devil."

He loomed in front of him, like Baal from before, only with a single monstrous head. His stature having risen since their last rendezvous, he appeared fifty feet tall.

"Am I dead?" asked No. 44.

"Yes and no," said the devil. "You blew your fucking brains out. But we still need you to finish what you started. Try as you might, you're in it till the end."

The devil gestured to a mirror, and No. 44 stood in front of it. He was a sickly sight: an anemic demon—all brittle bones. One horn busted, his lower extremities mangled, his skin yellow, his eyes hollow and black. He hissed at himself and recoiled.

"What am I?"

"An abomination, to be sure," said the devil. "But don't worry about it. Who isn't these days?"

The devil invited him to hang out and relax awhile, and No. 44 felt indebted to him. The devil was a good friend and understood No. 44's needs, and he showed him around and introduced him to some of the other tenants scattered around hell. He met some of the dukes and wandered around the rocky terrain; hell was a labyrinthine catacomb filled with intriguing locales—and one spot in particular drew No. 44's interest and fancy. It was a section with a little house surrounded by murky, green vegetation; giant alligators populated the creek running alongside its north-facing wall. He'd sit on a small balcony near the top of the house and watch the alligators swim by. He saw toads and lizards and frogs and found this to be a charming oasis. He spent most of his time there, and it reminded him of the house he'd grown up in. The devil would come by for a visit now and again, and No. 44 would sit on the balcony while the devil sat outside, and they'd sip tea and bask in the delight of the other's company.

He ate heartily and rested up, and slowly his weathered physique began to fill in; he checked himself out in the mirror and was happy to report that his looks, although still ghoulish, were mending. Soon he would get back to work. His vacation was coming to an end; the killings would resume.

102

"God, praise the madman with too much soul."

The devil showed him to the pod—a mushy, oozing pustule that could link him to the other side. Hell's Overman. *Disgusting*, thought No. 44. He would enter into it, climb inside and submerge into its folds. The devil told him to think of it like a giant flower enveloping him, giving him a big hug— but to No. 44, it felt more like being sucked on, salaciously digested, trapped in the mouth of some worm. The pod would move around and wiggle and cry out and whine...

He got inside, and much like the Overman, he wound up in dreams; only this time, he was the architect, except he was only able to draw up one set of floor plans, and his arena was permanent; he invited them inside, his lair reminiscent of the hell he was currently inhabiting or some crumbling castle's unorthodox lair (a wine cellar, perhaps?)—subterranean and stinking, but strangely romantic.

Samantha Stuart woke up at a candlelit table across from No. 44, and he said, "Good evening," and she said, "Who the hell are you?" and he said, "To hell with this," and he whacked her on the head with a sharp stone he'd recently come across, and then he was back and climbing out of the stinking pod. He emerged full of gunk. The devil asked him how it went, and he said, "What's done is done," and then he wandered back to the cottage with the alligators, and No. 44 realized that he liked hell very much. Perhaps he had found a more permanent residence at last.

103

It continued along in this fashion, with the devil going about his hellish duties and paying No. 44 frequent, casual visits. No. 44 went to the pod every few days and knocked off another murder, getting him one step closer to the end—that elusive one-hundredth kill. Would he miss this journey? He was curious what would become of his life once the project had come to completion. Where would he go? What would he do? He asked the devil while they sat enjoying some tea, but the devil said not to worry. His destiny was already written, embedded in the stone, flowing in the magma. He told him to resign himself to the no-plan plan for now. Things would go the way they were supposed to. No. 44 figured the devil was right, and he pushed his worries out of his mind, and he watched as an alligator devoured a goat that'd just tried to cross the creek; it shrieked and tumbled and was no match for the predator. The alligator ate and moved on. No. 44 sipped his tea, and one of hell's slaves brought him some kebabs and a liter of wine. It was another good day.

104

Billy Budd came by and met him at his candlelit table. He was number 84 on the list, and No. 44 was feeling conversational, and he asked Billy what he thought about his life. Was it satisfactory? What could be done to improve it? Billy was an insurance agent, married with two kids, and he said he was an ordinary enough fellow; he didn't ask for much, and what he got, he was happy to get. However, he was currently at odds with his wife; she belittled him and flirted openly in front of him with his coworkers (particularly Kenneth), and he had it on good authority that she was cuckolding him (and had been for quite some time)—but he still loved her even though he kind of hated her too, and No. 44 listened and probed around, and he asked Billy about his dreams and aspirations, and Billy mulled this over, and No. 44 got out his trusty rock and pummeled Billy with one swift blow. He emerged from the pod, a gunk-soaked ghoul, and then he ventured back to his cottage. He witnessed another of hell's sunrises and heard its heralding horn and went to bed at the dawn of a new day. He heard the alligators splashing around, and for supper, he ate a Philly cheesesteak.

105

One day, he met another of hell's occupants: Jacko. He was a disseminator of pain, a torture machine (aided by three fallen angels and two hellish titans); he catered to a certain style of sinner. It was under his knife that the greedy spent their afterlives—the most obnoxious of Gehenna's deep dwellers. He was a stand-up chap, as No. 44 would come to know. He would come by and bring a bottle or two of some stinking booze that he'd brewed himself in the bowels of his pit. He and No. 44 would get drunk and tease the alligators or go out and whip the sinners, or sometimes they'd just sit and swap stories and tell tall tales. Jacko was black all over and had a giant rack of horns—four in fact—darting out from the top of his head. He stood around the same height as No. 44, but his muscular stature offered a more intimidating monster. He said he liked hell but that he missed things, and when No. 44 asked him what kind of things he missed, he just shrugged and said, "The usual stuff."

Apart from Jacko, No. 44 hit it off with a gal named Naamah. She was a gorgeous demon; she was slender and curvaceous with ivory horns and a golden hue populating her scales. She and No. 44 had met through the devil, and the devil gave No. 44 a wink and a nudge as if to say, "Look at this beaut." She was a succubus and one of hell's most accomplished sexual deviants. She and No. 44 began a ravishing carnal relationship involving all manners of divergent and aberrant behavior, running the gamut of sodomitic and sadomasochistic practices, and even involving supernatural incantations and bizarre group sex scenes. They once incorporated a hypnotized alligator, using its scabrous physique as an unorthodox prop, propelling them in new directions with their lovemaking techniques.

She was fun too, and No. 44 had many good laughs along with many good comes in her company. Her vagina was cold, and No. 44 had the distinct sensation of entering an icy tomb each time he penetrated her. He saw her every few days, and although No. 44 and the devil never spoke of it, they both knew (on the sly) that each of them was currently in the fold of participants and partners and lovers in which Naamah shuffled through on a continual and habitual basis—her appetite outside the scope of any one individual.

No. 44 walked down from the house along the creek and went to the pod. Number 85 was waiting for him, and he jumped into the goo of the pod's mouth, and it took him away to that distant candlelit murder scene; Ted Dorsy sat across from him.

"How's it going, Ted?" asked No. 44.

But Ted didn't answer; he seemed very confused. Mercury was in retrograde.

106

"All errors eventually right their wrong, or 'til death do us part."

"It was a good grift," said Jacko, and then he pulled the trigger and blew apart Major Jordan Garnier's brains from two hundred yards out; he was looking through the scope of his bolt-action rifle, a direct hit; the man's skull and meat everywhere. No. 44 was looking through the binoculars at Jacko's success story.

"Well done."

The devil had sent his two pals on a sniper mission. A rogue agent had been discovered among hell's personnel, a mole working for the other side. "He's a loser disguised as a prize," said the devil. "Take that asshole Major Garnier out by any means necessary!"

When they got back (the deed accomplished), the devil had them over for dinner, and that night, he spoke of God, and he said, "God is the greatest nihilist of all. He needs nothing, wants nothing, and therefore believes in nothing." This resonated with No. 44, but perhaps it was wrong, and it was a trick cast by the devil's tongue, its eloquence coupled with his misguided morals might have crafted a tricky little spell—but perhaps none of it really mattered, anyway. Good and evil were only part-time occupations to No. 44: indifference was his natural state; evil was just what he got paid for.

The devil kept on about God, but then he switched his tune and said He was a good chap, a worthy opponent and, all in all, a good nemesis; deep down he even liked Him... nay, loved Him—he said this after many bottles of booze, and the trio praised the heavens and cheered on the hellfire. The next day, No. 44 puked on the floor, and he didn't get out of bed until dinnertime.

107

Number 86 was a zebra. It wasn't what No. 44 had expected, but in some ways, he had come to expect the unexpected. When he got to his usual arena, seated at the table, the zebra appeared in the corner. A beautiful animal. It looked at him with bemused curiosity and then just stood there while No. 44 sat; he stared at it for a long time, smoking cigarette after cigarette, taking in the contrast of its stripes and enjoying the exotic nature of the animal in his forlorn lair. He stayed cooped up in there for hours, and the zebra lay down, and eventually, it fell asleep. He waited and tiptoed over, holding his rock. It took two big hits. He lay down next to its corpse and closed his eyes. When he opened them, he was back in the pod; he climbed out and asked one of the slaves to fetch him a smoothie. He drank it and walked back to his abode; he saw Jacko and waved, and when he got back to the cottage, he passed out in his bed. He was exhausted; he didn't have anything left. The zebra had somehow gutted him.

108

"An evil man is often a strangely ambitious soul."

He dreamt he was back working at a large corporate office; faces from his past that he hadn't seen in years reemerged. He worked in a sector called "The Hip and the Heel." Everyone was dressed in a suit. And as the dream went on, No. 44 noticed that the building was falling into increasing disrepair. He saw water leaking down walls and rats scurrying around the hallways. He woke up mildly disgusted. He went for a walk. He heard a whimper and searched out its source. He saw trash bags and thought the sound might've come from some rats or vermin or one of those foot-long worms (with six carnivorous heads) that hell was so fond of... but he looked anyway. It was a dog—half dead, covered in shit, bleeding. He picked her up. She was trembling. He brought her to his house. He washed her and tended to her wounds. The dog slept with him that night, and in the morning, he gave her a name.

He cared for her and let her rest, and the dog took a few days before it was milling about as healthy dogs typically do. He fashioned a leash and a collar and took Else for a walk around hell's corridors. He brought the dog to see the devil, and the devil said, "Nice dog." Naamah was indifferent, and Jacko lifted her up, and the dog licked his face.

He tied the leash to a rock and got into the pod. He killed number 87 without paying much attention to his victim. They were a means to an end, and he wanted to get back to Else as fast as he could. But when he closed his eyes and tried to get out, nothing happened. "Hello!" he yelled. He heard a voice coming from an intercom saying that there were some technical difficulties, but not to worry, soon they'd have everything worked out. Then the devil came on and told him that they were sending him a suitcase, and he asked No. 44 if he'd stuff the body into it. The suitcase dropped down from a dark spot in the ceiling, and No. 44 said okay, but the suitcase wasn't big enough, and then an axe dropped down to facilitate his task.

When he finally got out (a silly glitch due to a temperamental pod), he asked the devil why he'd asked him to put the body in the suitcase, and the devil shrugged. "I just thought it'd give you something to do, something to pass the time." The dog looked at them and let out a small bark.

109

"A gun's just a remote for turning people off. It's yanking a cord from the outlet." Jacko was talking about death, and No. 44 asked Jacko what happens when you die in hell, and Jacko said that you get remixed and reborn in the goo at hell's lowest pit. Then you had to fight your way out, smashed and crushed under thousands of other newly repurposed souls trying to bust their way out too, a bucket of crabs each pulling at one another. No. 44 asked Jacko if he'd ever died in hell before... and he said once, a long time ago, and it took him ages to get out.

He took No. 44 to the pit he was referring to. It was so long and deep and dark that all No. 44 could see was the blackness; there was a hum, and Jacko said that the hum was the accumulation of screams and torment localized into a single sound coming from one horrible place. He asked Jacko if Major Garnier was down there, and he said he probably was.

No. 44 sat at home that night with Else and thought about Kevin Bacon and six degrees and how everyone was apparently related or connected through six people (or less) back on Earth, and he figured this was probably the same in heaven and hell (especially if lineage was accounted for), and he thought of how this separation took no account of good or evil, and how everyone was only six degrees from the greatest murderers and villains in history. He started thinking about ideas and about how ideas form, and he wondered if each idea was only separated by six others (the half-baked or fully-formed children of the ether) and how each desirable idea probably required an evil idea along its sequence or journey to get to, like monkey bars with a rung or two dipped in the devil's sauce, no sequence was without its killer or madman or villain (rare exceptions excluded). Chance or probability made it clear that the germ of each genius brainchild was stewed in a strange sequence of thoughts, and that each truly evil idea probably had a saintly vision somewhere along its rotten routes.

110

"The best you can hope for is a good run."

Some people look at heaven and see hell, and vice versa. This is what No. 44 told number 88 on his list, Kurt Jackson. Kurt said that No. 44 was probably right. When all was said and done, all that really mattered was perspective. That's what people are: walking perspectives. No. 44 concurred, and he and Kurt chatted for well over an hour, and No. 44 thought that he'd found an intelligent man and a new friend in Kurt, and then he remembered—he still had to kill him. And he did something he hadn't done in a long while; he spoke to his soon-to-be victim, and he told him what was about to happen. And Kurt asked if there was any way of changing his mind or altering his perspective, and No. 44 said that unfortunately there was not. So be it, said Kurt, and he closed his eyes, and he said to hell with it, and No. 44 whacked him on the head, and Kurt screamed, and it took four strong blows to crush his skull.

111

No. 44 was summoned to go meet with the devil the next day. He got to the devil's lair, which was large and open and had a pit that the devil liked to partially submerge in, his arms resting above, hell's primo tub, and the devil asked No. 44 how he was doing, and No. 44 said, "Good." The devil told him they had a bit of a problem—a technical fiasco, really; somehow, someone or something had poisoned the pods, and their network was down, perhaps permanently or, at any rate, for a long while. They would need to use an alternate and older and more medieval means of transportation to get No. 44 in contact with his victims. The devil asked No. 44 how many kills remained, and No. 44 said twelve.

Naamah entered the devil's lair, and pockets of air bubbled up from the devil's tub, and the devil told No. 44 that Naamah was going to teach him how to enter people's minds and muck about in their heads. It was an ancient practice that required a high level of skill, but the devil knew that

No. 44 was sharp enough to pick it up in record time. Naamah took him to a circular room with leather sofas, and she told him to sit. She said it was about mindfulness and concentration, and she asked him who was next on the list, but No. 44 didn't know, and she smiled through her irritation.

"All right, come back tomorrow with the list, same time, same place, and we'll get started then." No. 44 nodded and went home. Else greeted him at the door, and when he rounded the corner, he saw a pile of shit on the floor.

112

When he met Naamah the next day, she was seated in the exact same place in the exact same position, her only change, of course, being her attire; she wore a bright red dress. *God, was she lovely*, thought No. 44. They started up right away, and Naamah showed him how to concentrate, and she pictured the 89th victim, Charles Clark. When she did this, No. 44 noticed her eyes rolled back, and she hummed to herself, and then she spoke to No. 44 even though her eyes and demeanor were strange. She was plugged into Charles' brain (in her trance-like state). "I'm in. See, if you do this properly, you can theoretically be in two places at once. Operating a projection or a drone or a decoy, a capable killing or fucking or conversing machine, while still being seated on this here couch. You try."

She gave him the incantation, and he recited it in his head; at certain choice intervals, he was told to insert the name of the person he was seeking to infiltrate, and all the while, he should picture them as he declaimed the spell. No. 44 tried

Naamah's technique, but it didn't work. They practiced for three hours, and all No. 44 could muster was a brief flicker in which he thought he'd glimpsed or rushed into Charles' head—but he couldn't be sure. Naamah patted him on the back and said, "That's enough for today." He felt her disappointment as she said, "Good try."

113

No. 44 met Naamah the next day for another attempt at connecting to Charles Clark. The devil was standing outside the room when he got there, and the devil asked him how it was going, and No. 44 said okay. The devil told him not to worry and handed him two pills and told him to take them. "They'll take some of the edge off and ease in the process," said the devil. No. 44 swallowed the pills and used his saliva to flush them down, and then he greeted Naamah inside.

"Ready to get after it?"

"Sure, why not," said No. 44.

The pills seemed to energize him and help him focus, and although No. 44 was far from successful on his first go, about a half hour into their session, he felt the Overman-like sensation of being sucked through a tube—but like Naamah pointed out, he was still on the couch and could feel it beneath him even as he plugged into Charles' brain. It felt like an immersive videogame. And perhaps because of this thought, he envisioned himself as Pac-Man, gobbling up the landscape in a perpetual dark void. He saw Charles, or what he intuited he was, and went after him, trying to eat him up. Charles kept morphing between a human and a pixelated carrot (it was a strange series of events), and finally, No. 44 caught up with Charles and ate him, and then he felt himself relax and let go and be pulled out from Charles' head. The circular room came into focus, and Naamah was smiling back at him when his eyes rolled around. "Good work," she said, and then she kissed him on top of his head, and No. 44 sat beaming.

After he'd accomplished that first voyage (Overmanning without the Overman), he realized he could create or craft any environment he wanted—there was no limit to where he could go or what he could do once he'd plugged into the destination's head via that strange incantation and the appropriate channels of concentration. *It was a bit like swimming*, he thought, and once the gist was understood, the basic connection calibrated, one was able to stretch and contort the narrative as one saw fit—flow within it. He was a conjuror of ephemeral nightmares, where the threat of death and dismemberment were very real, and he was oh-so-giddy once he realized the strange possibilities this new skill offered him.

114

Jacko was waiting for him when he got back to his house; there was a worried look on his face. No. 44 asked what was going on, and Jacko stared mutely at the alligators outside, trying to mash the words around to properly manufacture the sentence he seemed to be straining to bring forth. He told No. 44 that something was amiss or off; some strange play was afoot. He said he couldn't put his finger on it, but he felt it. "I swear," he said.

No. 44 told Jacko to calm down, and he thanked his friend for his concern even as he became increasingly worried and paranoid himself. What strangeness was at play? What beast was galloping towards him? What plan was unfolding before his fiendish eyes? Perhaps he could ask the devil, but Jacko warned against it and said that the devil was at the heart of the mystery, the probable gooey center of the jigsaw. Jacko told No. 44 to keep his wits about him and his head on a swivel; he patted No. 44 on the back and left. And No. 44 sat petting Else, trying hard to keep his mind focused on possible conspiracies and the dangers that lay ahead. This proved to be rather difficult because all his mind wanted to do was leap off cliffs and soar into uncharted creative interzones—take flight with his new skill set.

He had one more session with Naamah the next day, their last together; it would be his 90th victim that he was plugging into today. He was feeling nostalgic, and after the mandatory incantation and the rushing forward into Becky Benedict's mind, No. 44 set the scene near his childhood home, on his front lawn, staring out at that wonderful little neighborhood. But once he got there, he realized how strange it was to set a murder there. He saw his old sandbox and the park across the street on the other side of the crescent and the large maple trees with their gnarled branches camouflaged with foliage. He heard kids playing and saw two of them near a teeter-totter. Becky was standing a few feet in front of him with her back turned; No. 44 asked how she was doing.

"Good," she said. "This place seems so familiar. Did I grow up here?"

"I don't think so," said No. 44.

Becky stood quietly; the mood of the place had overtaken her and something about the constructed milieu had un-earthed a bushel of feelings within; it was strong medicine—like the smell of her mom's living room or her ex-boyfriend's shampoo or the family car on a hot day or the smoldering remains of a backyard bonfire or her aunt Pamela's baked ziti.

No. 44 showed Becky around, and he got lost in his child-hood world; he conjured up old neighbors and sights, and he introduced her around. She was warm and welcoming and wonderful to be around. They stayed together talking for a long time... and No. 44 realized he couldn't kill her.

He wouldn't kill her now and, presumably, he would not kill her later. She was too precious; he could sense it. Maybe this was what Jacko was talking about. A left turn in the trajectory of the plot. Becky asked him for his name, and he said Jebediah Wells, and when he unplugged from Becky's head, Naamah was staring back at him with a stern look on her face.

The devil was outside the room when No. 44 left, and the devil asked him how it went, and No. 44 said, "Good." The devil asked him if he'd accomplished his goal, and No. 44 said, "Sort of." The devil restructured his query and asked if Becky was dead, and No. 44 said, "Not yet." *He paused.* "Were they in a rush?" and the devil said, "Yes."

At home, No. 44 sat thinking about what to do; he suddenly felt off and alone in hell, wanting only to return to Becky and his home, or his idea of home (however fabricated and half-formed). He would turn his back on the devil and Naamah and hell if he had to; he could feel his allegiance changing, all after one perfunctory hangout. His will or destiny had charted its course elsewhere. *How fickle are the loyalties of man*, thought No. 44.

115

No. 44 needed to come up with a plan. He could not do what he'd been asked or required. He'd killed a zebra, a kid, a demon, not to mention tens of other regular Joes and Janes and what-have-yous scattered across his bleak journey, and here he was stranded at Becky Benedict, without an oar to paddle with; the current was drifting his boat to some unknown port, and he knew he only had a limited amount of time to come up with a solution.

He decided to visit Becky again that night from the comfort of his bed. He heard the alligators snapping outside. He plugged in, and there she was. And then he had a thought and posed Becky a question: was she sleeping right now? And she said no and to come and have a look, and she backed into him and merged with him, and she gave him her eyes for a moment, and he saw the world blurring past through her perspective. *Windbreakers, sidewalks, an elementary school, redwood trees.* She stepped forward, and they were back in his old neighborhood. And he asked her what her biggest fear was, and she said, "To be consumed."

116

The next day, No. 44 went to see the devil. He would come clean, refuse further progress along the list. He opened the door to the devil's lair.

"Hey, devil."

"What's up, No. 44?"

"I can't do it anymore. I just can't kill Becky Benedict... I just can't."

"You're a real pain in the ass, you know that?" The devil looked at No. 44 and smiled. "I've been here a long time, kid, and I'm getting real tired—but I'll make you a deal. You're the best I've seen in a long while, a promising bastard with a knack for brutality, and if this is what it takes, so be it."

No. 44 stared, a bit confused, and the devil told him that it was okay. They'd wait it out. Becky was twenty-seven, and the devil told him that she'd die at forty-two in a freak accident while slipping down the stairs at a grocery store. That gave him fifteen years.

On his way back to his house, happy but a bit confused, No. 44 ran into Jacko, and he invited his friend over, and they drank and chatted, and No. 44 told Jacko about the new developments, and he told Jacko that everything would be all right. The problem was dealt with, but Jacko just shook his head.

It was the last time No. 44 saw Jacko. It was rumored that the devil had killed him, but he could have just run off to some unknown layer of hell, too. The scuttlebutt was numerous.

117

"The end of days was populated by people who couldn't endure the party. Those reluctantly burning out when they'd rather fade away."

So, No. 44 had a fifteen-year repose, a hiatus to be spent with Becky (which consequently elongated the lives of the other names on the list—an inadvertent kindness spilling out from our dear murderer to his future murderees). And although he wasn't able to leave hell physically, his mastery of the technique allowed him to plug into Becky Benedict's head and live a fulfilling life with the woman he loved. They saw magical sights together and constructed whole worlds blossoming forth from their imaginations, and No. 44 grew to understand and anticipate her tastes. They made love, and sometimes she would give him her eyes, and he would see the world again as she saw it. They made a home around the neighborhood he'd first taken her to, adjusting and renovating and conforming it to their whims and fancy. Two years into their relationship, Becky got pregnant. And No. 44 asked Naamah if this could happen, and Naamah said, "Of course." So Becky and No. 44 sired a son and bore him into the real world, and his name was Gottfried. No. 44 watched his little boy grow through the eyes of his lover, dreaming often of his son back on Earth.

"So, what should we do? Sail the seas? Deconstruct the Vatican? Open a butcher shop?"

"No, let's just sit for a while."

No. 44 drew up the floor plan, and he put them on an empty beach nestled in a thickly covered bed with pelts and duvets under a foggy morning sky. They listened to the sound of the waves, and No. 44 heard a dog bark somewhere in the mist. The horn of a ship sounded off, unseen in the haze, and No. 44 kissed the woman he loved, and then he asked if he could see his son, and she shuffled into him and merged, and he saw his little boy seated in his high chair at the dining room table, food smeared across his grinning face and all down his bib. No. 44 smiled: he was so happy it hurt.

In the early years, No. 44 would imagine Gottfried and project his image into his and Becky's simulated life. This only lasted a short while though because, as the boy grew, No. 44's projection could not account for all his blossoming idiosyncrasies; in other words, the boy's personality was taking shape, and the fabricated version was a blasphemous rendition of the boy's developing complexities. He would step into Becky's eyes as often as she'd allow and witness his son in all his splendor.

He'd only plugged into Gottfried's head once when the boy had been three. He held his smiling son, and he lifted the boy into the air, but he refused to do it again. It was too much for the demon. He couldn't bear the crushing weight of love that such a meeting entailed. The bird would remain locked in its cage. Restraint and distance were key.

One day, he asked Naamah who it was he was communicating with inside; was it the consciousness of the person, their soul, their unconscious? And Naamah said that it was an amalgamation, with the conscious side only somewhat aware of the visitor, only faintly, like the smallest, tiniest blur in the periphery. And No. 44 asked how he could kill or copulate and manufacture an offspring when everything inside was so malleable, and Naamah said, "The best way I can explain it is that you're interacting with their will, and however fickle or mercurial you might find a person, that kernel of who they are governs the entire vessel and remains steadfast. It's the core of the seed from which all else sprouts. When you're inside, you're plugged into the smallness of this holy thing—to the richness of whichever schmuck you're connected with. Steer it somewhere and the nervous system will find an appropriate response to the stimuli provided. And sometimes things bleed through, between the two spheres, like an overlapping slit with a small opening, and microscopic things might pass between."

118

Becky was back with her old boyfriend. This had happened before. Who she was out in the physical world was miles away from the woman No. 44 spent his days with inside. He doubted if that portion of Becky even knew who he was, and if it did, it was like Naamah had said, only as a faint flicker.

He'd asked her once if she knew how she'd gotten pregnant, and she said that of course she did, and she smacked him for asking such a silly question, but he continued and asked if she knew—and he pointed at the sky—outside of here. And Becky said that she accepted the strangeness of it out there; she wasn't one to ask futile questions but to deal with the blows as they came in; a broken condom was the presumed cause of the genesis of her baby. He asked if he could see his son, and she blushed, and she said not now, and he asked her why, and she said because she was spending time with Dean at the moment (current boyfriend and mistaken paterfamilias). No. 44 understood that it was stupid to get jealous—he was married to the inner sanctum of

Becky, to the bare, pallid pulp of her being, not to her outer skin—but as she slept, he cuddled up to her and merged with her and got a glimpse through her eyes. And he saw Dean and her banging away ("Oh, Dean! *Don't stop*. Fuck me, Dean!"), and he lost it and got deplorably upset. He even witnessed it all from her POV, i.e., as if *he* was being fucked by Dean. He exited Becky's head, and he sat alone in hell for a long time. Else made a small yelp and then continued to snore. He plugged into Dean's mind an hour or so later. He went in with guns blazing; he colored himself as a previous version, a chainsaw for one hand and a .38 in the other, and he went to work, and it was fast and quick, and before a minute was up, Dean's corpse was a pulverized mess of fluids and limp musculature.

When he returned to Becky the next day, she was furious. He tried to tell her he had nothing to do with it, but she knew. For a month, she refused to talk to him. He tried to win her back by taking her on majestic trips, psychedelic odysseys, and romantic journeys down the rabbit hole of his imagination, but nothing worked: time was needed. And slowly and gradually, things returned to their former ways, and No. 44 had to promise to keep his rottenness at bay. He promised he would—staring into her beautiful brown eyes— when, in fact, the best he could muster was a good college try.

119

He hoped his son would not become a guttersnipe or a flake or a pushover or a bullying buffoon as he grew older. He expected phases, sure—but he didn't want his son going off the rails into treacherous terrain. It was difficult to watch him grow in glimpses without any kind of direct contact or supervision (forever stuck in hallowed hell); he wanted to help guide the boy's ship, but this was difficult and required Becky as an intermediary. What he'd provided was the seed, supplying an aspect of the boy's nature, but nurture was beyond what he could ever deliver, and No. 44 was disheartened with his lack of influence over the boy's life.

The years wore on, and their son turned ten. Gottfried was a fine lad as far as No. 44 could tell, and his and Becky's relationship had somehow thrived amongst all the pitfalls, but time was sneaking up on them; they had two or maybe three years before it all evaporated, and the bridge connecting No. 44 to this life finally up and disappeared. He spent most of his time alone in his house and was rarely seen in hell and was considered a recluse and a hermit by most of those living there. One night, he spilled the beans and told Becky how she was going to die (words precipitating the event), and she kissed him and said that it was all right. She was happy, and whatever was going to happen would happen. She made him promise that he'd take care of Gottfried after she was gone, and No. 44 nodded and kissed Becky and rested his head on her shoulder, and she let it lie there for a long time.

He felt it, which was strange, like an electric shock. He was sitting in his living room, and then pop, like a switch going off. And he felt empty and strange and dazed. He tried to plug into her head, but he couldn't. He sat in his chair, not sure what to do. He got dressed and wandered over to the devil, and the devil just nodded and offered his condolences, and No. 44 asked where she'd gone, and the devil pointed upward, and then he was quiet, and then the devil said that No. 44 should get some rest. Tomorrow was a new day. He went home, and he thought of Else, his dead dog, and he thought of Becky and Gottfried, and then he tried to sleep, but he just lay there, clouded by grief and resignation, his horned head struggling with abnegation, unable to push forward, unable to fall apart or escape in dreams.

120

He felt eaten and broken and torn and tired and done with it all. The next day, he plugged into his son's head for the first time since the boy had been three. He tapped him on the shoulder.

"Who the hell are you?" asked Gottfried.

"I'm your pop."

Gottfried stood mute, mixing up his memories and the logic of the statement with the current predicament he found himself in. No. 44 had chosen to take the boy to the home he and Becky had created for themselves. He'd imagined it just as they'd left it, for his son's benefit and maybe for some of his own. Gottfried looked at No. 44 and then at the surrounding architecture of the scene.

"Where are we?"

"Your mom and I used to live here."

The boy had grown—and awkwardness had followed him, a gangly youth going on thirteen, and No. 44 could intuit the anger and brutishness that flowed through his veins coursing through those of his son. He smiled at him, asked how he was doing, and the boy said he was fine. No. 44 told him to be steady, to keep his chin up, and that he'd be around if anything came up, and Gottfried let out an inarticulate reply, and No. 44 sneezed, then smiled and unplugged from his son's head. He went and spoke with the devil afterwards; the devil looked thin and frail, and the devil told No. 44 to get on with the list. Ten kills remained, he said. "Now, hurry up, *will ya?*"

121

He got to work quickly; he wanted to get down to brass tacks, and he entered the mind of his 91st kill the next day, Donna Winkertips. He put her in a large landfill filled with smashed cars, and just as she was getting her bearings (she saw a rat; then she followed her gaze up to a stack of crushed SUVs, and then she pulled back and saw the rows upon rows of manufactured debris piled fifty feet high, one on top of the other, creating a sculptural maze of metallic design), she heard a great big baritone yell, and a beast with the head of a bull barreled forth from the darkness of the junkyard; brandishing a curved blade, the beast swung and sliced her in two, and although the shock was great, she'd barely had enough time to register fear or dread as No. 44 came out slashing—shearing with his scimitar—rushing her head-on.

He was soon lying in his bed, alone and tired without any thrill left for the hunt.

122

He spoke with the devil the next day and asked if there was anything he could do for his son, if there was any way to keep an eye on him, and the devil told him to plug into him, and No. 44 asked if there was any way he could go back to Earth since the boy was all alone now, and the devil shook his head. "It's a hard-knock life," said the devil, "and unfortunately, your boy will have to tough it out." *All by his lonesome...* thought No. 44. All by himself.

No. 44 plugged into his son as often as he could; they played catch and talked about Gottfried's life, and Gottfried would give No. 44 his eyes sometimes, just as his mother had done, and No. 44 would glimpse the boy's life: the school cafeteria, the teenage parties, class. He saw his boy play his championship baseball game from Gottfried's own perspective, and this gave No. 44 a great thrill. He wished he could do more, be a more active father in his son's everyday life, but hell was not easily escaped from. He'd killed numbers 92 to 97 in much the same manner as Donna

Winkertips, and he hadn't seen the devil since he'd sought his counsel about returning to Earth—his kills were all conducted from the comfort of his unmade bed. He rang for one of his slaves and asked for a cup of coffee. He bathed and brushed his pointed teeth and exited his house for the first time in over a week.

He went and saw the devil and told him that only three kills remained. The devil let out a sigh of relief, and No. 44 noticed that he had trouble breathing (a wheeze followed by a hiss and then a cough—performed with theatrical élan). An apparatus had been set up with tubes and a mask that the devil placed sporadically against his mouth; it ran to a large tank with dials being operated by little dwarfish hellions—a rendition of hell's diminutive iron lung. And the devil spat out a big loogie.

"Good, good," said the devil—*laboring with the weight of the vowels.*

"What's wrong?" asked No. 44.

"Never you mind, just keep to the task."

123

A goat was lying on the road; he was halfway home, and he stopped and examined the creature with its heavy panting. He wondered if it was injured or asthmatic (irregular breaths abounding that day), but then it happened, and a kid burst forth—just popped out, and the goat gave birth, and the newly arrived offspring lay in the dirt, and then it tried to steady itself and rise. No. 44 stroked its mother and told her everything would be okay, and then he left and walked on and let the rest of the scene play out without him. At home, he ate and watched the alligators roam outside. *Three kills left*, he thought. And yet, the end didn't feel like the end; it lacked resonance and nearness. It felt just as it'd always felt for as long as he could remember. A constant grind forward, with narrow glimpses of imagined hope, brief moments of possibility frittered away under the weight of reality. He wondered what was happening to the devil, but only for a moment, and then his thoughts returned to his son, and he lay in bed and plugged into Gottfried's head. It was the best drug he had going for him.

He planned to kill the last three assholes the next day. Soon it would all be over.

124

He woke up and had his coffee, and then he plugged into Norm Gladwell's head. They were on a dark country road (middle of the night); a tilting wooden fence ran along the narrow roadway half-buried under the snow. Norm asked where they were, and No. 44 said, "Who cares." Norm requested a cigarette, and No. 44 imagined a pack and withdrew his creation from his breast pocket and handed one to Norm. He lit it for him, and then Norm commented on the penumbra of stillness, the reek of calmness. They watched the snowdrifts, and No. 44 let Norm finish his smoke before he shot him.

After lunch, No. 44 continued on, riding the routes into Judith Pumpernickel's noggin. They were near the edge, and she seemed scared, less because of the demon and more so because of the setting. The jungle could be a frightening place. He pushed her into the water (a jaguar stared at them from the far bank of the Amazon), and he jumped in after her; she screamed as she rode along, closing in on the falls.

She went over first, and then No. 44 went over (thinking of fathers and shotguns and suicides). He unplugged himself in free fall at the very last instant and returned to hell with only one kill left after supper.

<h1 style="text-align:center">125</h1>

In the afternoon, he plugged into his son's brain. Gottfried's birthday was fast approaching. The boy would soon be thirteen. This was a happy time underlined by growth spurts and mysterious hard-ons, and he could see from the way the boy spoke of his life that he was in a good place. His grandparents had taken over his guardianship, cooking him roast beef dinners—the TV blaring, forgotten hearing aids misplaced in dusty old drawers. No. 44 kept it brief, and he told his son he loved him and that he'd see him soon. "Take care," he said, and he patted the boy on the back and ruffled his hair and returned to hell to finish the job.

He ate ribs that night and had a bottle of wine, and the slaves brought him his pipe. He felt sluggish and lazy and asked for coffee. He would soon kill Daniel Reever, the final fellow, and this strange journey would have its denouement, its end; *and finally*, he thought, *I can be at peace or rest or die or lie in bed for another fucking decade.* His life had become a series of poorly directed commercials, slotted between awful TV shows ("Oh, the MAYHEM!"), murder its flagship product, his product, his serviceable gift, "Oh, the glitz... Oh, the glam," pieced together on channel 47, running wild, broadcast twenty-four seven—where nobody was looking.

126

He placed Daniel in a hotel just off the main drag in a town he barely recognized. It was full of half-digested details and blurry characteristics, declining in its half-life. He had Daniel in the hallway on the ground floor, and he saw the entranceway to the pool on his left, and through the small rectangular window on the door, he saw kids and parents splash and make their way from one end to the other. The ice machine made its racket, and No. 44 said, "What's up, Daniel?" But Daniel didn't answer—he looked at No. 44, and then No. 44 noticed that Daniel wasn't who he thought he was or how he'd pictured him. He was now a lady, and then a kid, and then he was a Black man, and then an Asian woman, and then a White dwarf; he had a mustache, and then he was obese, and then he was a frail old spinster.

"What the hell's going on?"

"It won't work in here," said Daniel. "Go see the devil."

No. 44 stood staring at the shapeshifter, and the children raged on, splashing and yelling in the pool.

He unplugged from Daniel's head, and still a bit drunk from the wine, he wandered over to the devil's lair. The devil greeted him with a smile; he looked worse still, emaciated and weak, clavicles jutting out, and No. 44 asked him what was going on. The last kill (Daniel Reever) seemed aware of some blueprint, ready for him, was cloaked in some intricate suit or under some impressive arrangement.

"Come and sit," said the devil. "Do you know what you've accomplished?"

"No."

"You've passed the test, kid. You've finally done it. Every couple hundred years or so, we test someone out, few make it, either due to defects in their design or a lack of stamina or will, and you, Jebediah Wells, have conquered the task set before you. I offer you my respect and my congratulations."

No. 44 stood, waiting, the air of confusion thick, and the devil laughed.

"I am Daniel Reever, or at least I was. And now, you see, you are here to finish the job."

127

The task had been designed for the dukes and lieutenants of hell, but the devil told him that his application had caught their eye. They had tested him, and he was nearing the end of the process. And he'd done it... few believed he would (even the devil had his occasional doubts), but in due time, No. 44 had triumphed over the task, and here he was at its endpoint, ready to take up the throne...

"You'll need to eat me," said the devil. "That's how it ends."

And so, with some reservation, No. 44 accepted his new post (King of the Underworld), and he and the devil shook hands, and then the minions presented him with a gift: a specially crafted axe. He was to wield it against the devil and then set upon the morsels and gobble up the bits. The minions tied off the devil's right arm and crafted a pre-emptive tourniquet around his right shoulder as No. 44 was told to ready his swing. He looked at the devil who nodded his head. No. 44 leaned back and put the full thrust of his weight behind it, and he chopped, and he chopped, and he passed through flesh and bone, circulatory vessels and mangled meat, and off went the devil's right arm.

The minions administered pain medication to the devil, who smiled through the drugs and coughed up blood. No. 44 asked for some salt and a glass of beer, and then he dug in, cutting and skewering the devil's right arm with a knife and a fork; he ate as much as he could. He was feeling very full; supper had been a rich and decadent affair (and the devil's meat was no easy mouthful). But he kept at it, and bite by bite, he got there. The right arm along with all its tendons and ligaments and bony protuberances were all being ingested; whether raw or cooked or ground up and broken down, all meat and cartilage were run through the sporting channels of No. 44's gut.

The devil seemed to be bloating. It was strange. As No. 44 cut through the devil's left arm and ate, he noticed a rotundness to the devil beginning to take shape. He was fattening up heartily around his midsection and jowls. Each limb untethered offered a good four-hundred-pound increase to the remaining mass. He was an obese torso and head without arms and only one remaining leg. No. 44 felt bad and apologized to the devil, but the devil only responded in gobbledygook as his brain had deteriorated due to the concoctions the minions were forcing through his veins and nasal cavity.

No. 44 was tiring, and after seven days and seven nights, he'd cut through and eaten the entirety of the devil's arms and legs. He was in a constant state of pain and lethargy, running often to the bathroom to evacuate his bowels and then returning to finish off more of the meat. When the time had finally come to eat the devil's heart and head and belly, No. 44 made the devil look him in the eye, and he said,

"Goodnight, sweet prince." He kissed him on the forehead, and he swung his axe and planted it in the devil's skull. The devil slumped over as drool and blood seeped down his face and along his chest—his eyes unfocused; each rolled to the side.

128

It took No. 44 another week to finish off the rest of the devil. The minions helped prepare the meat and stuffed the devil into little meat pies. By the end, No. 44 could barely move, and he fell asleep and slept for days as his body fought to break down the devil's game. When he woke up, the job completed, the minions sang his praises and hailed his ascension.

He ran to the bathroom.

"Arise, No. 44! Arise, Jebediah Wells! Arise, devil! Arise and meet your fate!"

129

And so, No. 44 was the new devil. Over the coming days, new horns sprouted from his head, and his physique mutated to accommodate its new alchemy. He noticed that he could easily shift his body, morphing like sand or ooze into any shape he pleased, hardening and softening at will. He was a sly fox and a cunning son of a gun—transforming into anything he dared dream up. He called for Naamah, who bowed as she entered, and she congratulated him on his latest achievement.

She asked him what kind of king he wanted to be. He was silent: he didn't know how to answer that.

130

And so, the devil adapted to his task, overseeing hell and all its minutiae. And one night, early in his tenure, the devil had a wonderful dream; he relived his life and all its accompanying joys and sorrows and pain; and through this elliptical journey, he understood something about who he was and what he was and what type of king he could possibly be, and when he woke up and the minions asked him how he'd slept, he told them that he'd slept beautifully. He asked for Naamah, and when she came by his lair, he asked her to repeat the question... the same question from before (when he'd first laid his ass on the much-coveted seat)—the one concerning the type of king he wished to be, and so she asked him the same question one more time.

And No. 44 looked at her and smiled, and he was gleeful in his response, resplendent in his display.

"My dearest Naamah, I know who I am and what type of king I shall be. I'm a sadist, a sensationalist, an artist, and a lowbrow fiend. I am the king, the devil—a sage for the unclean.

I am a pirate and a tramp and a vicious little whore. But by and large, and most of all, I am a creator, a prognosticator, a pornographer... a diabolical drugstore."

And Naamah smiled.

"And now it is time for us to create another loop," said the devil.

And the minions all laughed and rejoiced; *and so it begins again*, thought the narrator, and another masterwork was beginning to form, and the momentum carried them over the edge, and they fell towards worlds unknown, towards adventure, towards uncertainty, towards erections and lubrication, towards suicidal ermines, sugary mountaintops, long locks, gangrene... and the devil felt extraordinarily lucky and grateful to all involved. And the next day, back on Earth, a bomb went off, and thousands died, and a marching band was organized to welcome the new sinners, and one of the sinners said to another one, "Is this hell?" and the devil overheard him, and the devil said, "No, son, this is just one of life's *many* cellars." This made one or two of the new recruits smile, and they walked on. And the devil sat on his throne, watching the grand march, and the horns sounded, and the drums rolled, and the devil picked his teeth with a rib bone and scratched at an itchy, low-hanging testicle.

He smiled; he was happy. Hell was all right.

www.ingramcontent.com/pod-product-compliance
Lightning Source LLC
Chambersburg PA
CBHW021306190726
48288CB00003B/724